RUFF COUNTRY

Tales West by Southwest

FIRST EDITION

ISBN 0-9624499-3-8

Library of Congress Catalog Card Number 94-69822

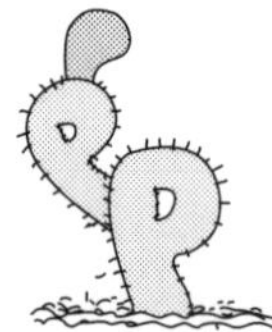

The Prickly Pear Press
P.O. Box 42, Payson, AZ 85547

Ruffly Proofed by Nancy Dedera

Design & Production
by W. Randall & Deirdre A. Irvine
Randy's Art Works! / Great Characters!

For Pablo

RUFF COUNTRY

Tales West by Southwest

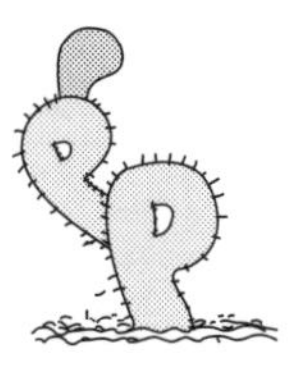

The Prickly Pear Press
P.O. Box 42, Payson, AZ 85547

CONTENTS

Ruff Illustration by Vincent Holbey

Ruffing It in Yavapai County

Most of the happenings and attitudes described in this little book transpired or developed in Yavapai County, Arizona. All the essays are the works of Lester Ward Ruffner. A native of the county seat and old territorial capital, Prescott, Budge Ruffner descends from several generations of Yavapai independent spirits who date back to frontier times.

The why of it is hard to explain, but undeniably certain geopolitical arenas give rise to an inordinate abundance of wry, wise and witty tales. When such a locale has a faithful and sensitive penman of the likes of Budge Ruffner, the reading world is blessed indeed.

Any competent storyteller, even a rank outsider, can acquire material in Yavapai County. Much of the land is national forest, generally unpeopled but enlivened by numerous wild and domestic creatures. Of lofty, conifer-clad mountains, brushy hardscrabble mesas, sculptured canyons, heart-stopping rims, and eventful streams, Yavapai builds its modern, second century American lifestyle upon chronicles of pioneer ranching and boomtime mining. Prescott, the Mile-High City, is a feature writer's prayer come true: "Robert Groom was the first surveyor. And while it is said he placed a spot of phosphorous on his dog's tail to guide him home from Whiskey Row each night, he was able to lay his streets straight come morning." Prescott might have remained the Arizona capital, but according to legend, an early-day legislature narrowly voted for Phoenix when a Prescott booster failed to answer roll call. He couldn't attend that day's session because a lady-of-the-evening had swallowed his glass eye. (When she mistakenly chugalugged a bedside tumbler of water containing it.)

Prescott's first saloon was set beside Granite Creek, "but the sight of water made the customers sick." So the building was moved to Montezuma Street. Others followed. Hence, the nickname, Whiskey Row. An early-day visitor jotted in his diary, "Last night I was in a billiard saloon here. A game of monte was going on in one corner, brag-poker in another, and a couple of dogs were having a free fight under the billiard table. I lived in Boston once for some time, but have no recollection of seeing anything exactly like that!"

The town's first eatery boasted of a deluxe menu: fried venison and chili for breakfast; roast venison and chili, and chili and beans for lunch; and from 4 o'clock on, plain chili for supper. To complement its community character, Prescott for a long spell had one of the West's more vitriolic broadsiders, John H. Marion. A sample, regarding a pacifist Indian agent, "We ought, in justice to our murdered dead, to dump the old devil into the shaft of some mine and pile rocks upon him...." Prescott sponsored arguably the very first public cowboy competition in 1888, and has put on a bigtime rodeo nearly every summer since. Most of Prescott's business district went up in smoke in the Great Fire of 1900, but before the ashes cooled, the roulette wheels were spinning in temporary shelters on the courthouse square. The sheriff served as treasurer. Once in a blocked-off

Prescott street a cowboy successfully rode a ton of furious bull bison for $100 in gold. Whenever Barry Goldwater ran for national office—including the Presidency—he announced from Prescott's courthouse steps. From such evocative origins, 30,000-population Prescott today prides itself in being a cultural center (acclaimed bronze statuary everywhere), retirement retreat, architectural showcase, recreational getaway, and operating address of on-line entrepreneurs who can live and work anywhere they choose.

All this provides grist for tales, easily come by. But it takes a homebred insider like Budge to depose upon the resurrection of a dead horse named Willow, tell about a highway robber who stuck up a road grading machine, and itemize the probate of a cowboy's estate beside a roundup campfire.

Ruffner was born on St. Patrick's Day, 1918, just six years into Arizona's statehood, the son of a prominent undertaker, Lester Lee Ruffner, and his wife, Mary Ward, the territory's first public school music teacher. The closest an older sister could pronounce "brother" was "budge," and the nickname stuck. The boy did poorly in school until he was enrolled in Phoenix's Brophy Preparatory, where strict Jesuit priests taught him to study to remember, read to think, and write to inform, persuade and amuse.

By Budge's own reckoning, his two most formative, mid-'teen summers were passed as Model A Ford driver and camp ("broken yoke, burnt bacon") cook for expeditions led by Barnard College anthropologist Gladys Reichard for field studies in Navajoland in and beyond Northeastern Arizona. In the early 1930s America's largest Indian reservation, the size of West Virginia, largely resisted the so-called progress of the greater nation. Navajos dwelt in six-sided or octagonal hogans of logs and mud. They shepherded flocks. And traveled, if at all, by foot, horseback, and wagon.

Scattered government schools and hospitals provided the bare beginnings of education for the young and marginal medicine for the neighboring. But the nearest commercial connection for most Navajos was the trading post, typically a one-story stone huddle housing a limited stock of food staples, yardage goods, and hardware (elsewhere in America quickly vanishing) such as horsecollars, fleecing shears and axe handles. Local economies operated on a monetary system of silver-turquoise pawn and store credit. Wool represented a main cash crop. An added value accrued when woven by hand into a unique fabric. As a kid Budge bought a splendid double saddleblanket for $2.50.

He also sat by the hour around the evening warming fire listening to Doctor Reichard sermonize against white ethnocentrism, and promote greater appreciation for an Athapaskan tribe that had prevailed—their value system, arts, matriarchal order, religion and language intact—through centuries of foreign invasion and cultural stress.

"She taught me," recalled Budge, sixty years later, "to judge people by their standards and not my own."

Several years of Army Air Corps service in World War II interrupted his college years at Loyola University, Los Angeles, and the University of Cincinnati. There followed decades of duty in the family mortuary business, thwarting somewhat his ambition to research history, write professionally and teach. Yet he did allot time to place stories in regional journals and author several books. He counts as most gratifying his stints as adjunct professor of Southwestern history and literature at Prescott and Yavapai colleges.

As his interest and equity in the mortuary

diminished, he plunged fulltime into what he characterizes as "not so much as a new life, but a metamorphosis into an entirely different human being." He accepted appointment to several state commissions, served two terms as president of the Arizona Historical Society, and joined trailblazing archeological surveys, notably a helicopter reconnaissance of the Grand Canyon. He reviewed books for *Arizona Highways* magazine and filled a page for the *Arizona Attorney* monthly of the state bar association. On and off, mostly on, his column has appeared in the *Prescott Courier* newspaper since 1964.

Curmudgeon, Budge is not. Although one senses now and then in his writing a nagging concern that a man in his seventies should cultivate a churlish streak. Fortunately for us all, there is not an irascible atom in his psyche. So when Budge takes an occasional ol' boy swipe at Yuppies, non-traditional cuisine and faddish fashions, the apology comes hard on the heels of the insult. For if Budge is anything as a soul and a writer, he is a generous, gracious and gentle man, and a hopeless sentimentalist. Budge can't claim, in the manner of Will Rogers, that he never met a man or woman he didn't like. But even within the unlikable, Budge tries to perceive redeeming worth. And upon devining a nugget of human goodness, he tends to overflow. Farewells, for him, are always misty affairs.

As one of his daughters has said:

"Father weeps when we send out his laundry."

Then what are we to do with this huge, western-dressed *hombre* with a laugh loud enough to fell ponderosa pines? Who lurches through social gatherings, shamelessly bragging about his honored historian wife, Elisabeth, their three children and eight grandchildren, one-of-a-kind cronies, his sassy and sometimes snooty hometown, its surrounding countryside, and the hosts of Indians, Jews, Mexicans, Slavs, Blacks—ministers, murderers, politicians, priests, lawmen, sainted and painted ladies—fools, leaders, connivers, gamblers and achievers—that he has met in the flesh or encountered in history? How must we deal with this man who has transmogrified into a veritable bifurcated volcano of anecdote? What to do with this minstrel who into his eighth decade continues to commit to paper his discoveries and ideas?

At least he is a living treasure of Yavapai County. Probably of Arizona. Possible of the nation.

Why... let us *enjoy* him!

Don Dedera
Payson, Arizona
November, 1994

CHAPTER

Rounding Up The Ruff String

You may have to turn off the main highway and creep over a rutted road for a few miles before you even see one. There are only a few left. These are free souls who still live and work like the ones who were part of the West that was.

The one I saw and talked with was a woman, named Adeline. In far Northern Arizona, where the tablelands are eroded into multicolored monuments, windows, bridges and escarpments, my companion and I had paused for lunch at the Vermilion Cliffs Bar & Grill aside U.S. Alternate Route 89. We asked directions to a historic rock shelter used for a winter by Frederick Dellenbaugh, an artist, boatman and topographer with the second Powell expedition down the Colorado River and through the Grand Canyon in 1871. We wanted to photograph the ruin.

"You better go up that road careful like," warned our waitress. "Adeline is liable to level a gun on you."

So slow and careful we went. And as predicted, Adeline had her 1873 Army .44-caliber Colt's pistol close by. Normally, we had been told, she would be atop a sixteen-hands-high horse. But this day she was sitting on a log, basking in the sun. Adeline was not unlike a dinosaur bone: difficult to judge her age, but certainly of another time. I guessed, seventy-five, maybe eighty.

Her thin body bore evidence of accidents considered inevitable for people who handle horses and cattle in rocky country. Fractures of the femur and pelvis had left her left leg several inches shorter than the right. She had the short leg stretched out, sort of displayed like a badge of honor. The left boot was built up, and was as battered as the leg. Her denim clothing was months removed from a laundromat.

We told her of our mission.

"You won't have no trouble crossing the wash and you will damn sure know when you get there 'cause the road ends."

With her eyes she invited us to "stay and chew the fat." She seemed more happy than hostile with the surprise visit by people wearing western hats like hers and dusty boots.

Adeline's camp lay beneath the western end of the Vermilion Cliffs, a thousand-foot-high, near-vertical wall of red, green and orange stone. The whole world along the Utah border appeared to be chemically defoliated. The dwelling of Adeline was an old pickup camper with an added-on wing, once a horse trailer. A mule and seven gaunt horses stood swatting flies in a nearby corral. Out of sight in the vast rangeland Adeline's few beef cattle grazed. When she needed a little cash, she'd sell one. She didn t sell very often.

We kept the conversation on a high plane. We knew instinctively that Roosevelt (Teddy, not Franklin) was the last president she approved of. The bark of a long-haired mongrel dog filled in the awkward pauses.

"Busted my leg when a horse pinned me up against the fence," she told us, then volunteered, "If I ever get hurt again, I don't want to be hauled off to no hospital. I'll take care of it right here by myself, and if that's the way my luck runs, I'd rather die here."

Likely, lacking a telephone, she wouldn't have much choice. The folks down along the highway had an understanding with a helicopter ambulance to fly them, in emergencies, to the hospital at Page, forty-five miles east. But Adeline had nothing but her truck.

Infrequently she would drive her old pickup at a steady thirty-five mph the eighty miles to buy supplies at Kanab, Utah, population 3,000. Adeline said she didn't mind the trip, but hated Kanab.

"Too many people, too crowded," she explained.

With her permission we drove on, found the shelter, located its spring, and took pictures of names and dates encised into boulders. Many of the marks were those of pioneer Mormon colonizers.

Our goals accomplished, we backtracked to Adeline's camp. She was still perched on the log, taking in the sun. Only now her pistol and rifle were out of sight. We tarried again, to say proper farewells. Maybe it was at a moment when my sidekick and I looked around and surveyed the pack of scruffy dogs, the string of drawn-up mounts, the humble shelter. Adeline blurted:

"I'm happy here. I have everything I need."

We never asked about her last name, where she came from, whether she ever had a family, if she owned the land, or why and how she chose the solitary life. When you're in the Old West, you know better than to raise personal questions.

The next few days were eventful with sensations of Zion National Park, Virgin Canyon and Las Vegas. But they didn't compare to Adeline.

There are still a few left out there, off the main highway. But not many. It's worth a lot of rocky road to find someone like Adeline.

© 1994 Bill Ahrendt

A bad way, it was, to get the message. In the upper left-hand corner of the envelope was my return address and next to it was the post office stamp, a finger pointing, "Return To Sender," and the reason checked: "Deceased."

I have no idea how old Carl Chukima was — that had been one of the problems when I tried to help him qualify for Social Security. He was born in Oraibi, Arizona, the ancient mountaintop capital of the Hopi Indian nation. He was a traditional Hopi, a ceremonial priest, a combat veteran of World War II, and the proud possessor of a Silver Star for valour and an old copy of *Life* magazine with a cover picture of him when he was awarded the medal.

He was my friend for almost fifty years. I have a Kachina (doll representing a Hopi god) in my home that I watched him carve from cottonwood root. A red, blue and green dance rattle that he made hangs on my study wall. A *paho* (prayer feather) he sent me last Christmas keeps my car accident-free. He has given me a great deal, but his greatest gifts are my appreciation of his ways and, above all, understanding.

Three times he asked me for money. Once he was hungry. The *pahos* had done little for his peach trees that year. Once he went to the State Fair and needed a bus ticket home. Once he got drunk in Winslow (maybe more than once) and when the policeman arrested him, he used language he had learned in the Army. That time it was $50, but I got a *paho* every Christmas. When I visited the Indian country, I slept in his ancient rock house, an honored guest — always near the stove — and I ate mutton stew at his clean pine table.

Like many American Indians, Carl suffered from trachoma, which stole away his eyesight as the years passed. But he never failed to plant his corn every year and tend his fruit trees, optimistically rooted in the sandy soil near his native village. From time to time, the Whipple VA Center Hospital at Prescott would provide sensitive and expert care when he could be persuaded to request it.

Despite his failing health, he always appeared on his village plaza for the ceremonials. These gave faith and hope to his life, and the one he knew would follow. This was Hopi-ness — the cornmeal, the drums, the flutes and the green cottonwood headbands, signals of summer, perhaps everlasting ones.

His last few years were eased by the Social Security check. His interview and qualification was a strange process for a Hopi. A kind and patient clerk handled it for him. She had to go by the book, asking questions that were difficult to answer from a Hopi point of view.

Who owns your pueblo?

"I was born in it; it must be mine," was the only Hopi answer.

How old is your house?

I pointed out that pottery shards indicate Oraibi was occupied some time before A.D. 1150; a title search would be difficult.

Carl had worked for a time for a road contractor and as a forest firefighter. These credits, together with his Army time, and a helpful government employee, gave him the dignity he deserved.

Now a frail old Hopi man has been placed in the red earth he loved. He has all the things he will need for his journey — a bowl, a blanket, some ceremonial objects and a bag of sacred cornmeal. His sister has a new American flag.

In beauty it is begun
In beauty it is finished
Go in beauty

Stump Duncan wasn't what you would call a social butterfly. He was a good cowboy who lived and worked fifty miles from town. He went to work at the 7UP Ranch, owned at the time by the Hill family in Camp Wood, Arizona.

He was the only steady cowboy the Hills hired. He had come to them from his home in West Texas when he was just a boy. His dimensions were about equal, five feet four, by five feet four; a compact hand, agile and strong. He went to work at the 7UP at the turn of the century, when a horse was the primary means of a cowboy's transportation, and trips into town for infrequent orgies usually resulted in disaster.

One early winter, when roundup was finished, Stump asked for a few days off to visit Prescott and take care of some personal matters. He borrowed one of the ranch horses named Willow, a favorite of the Hills. With his Levi's pockets bulging with his wages, Duncan two days later arrived in Prescott and put his horse up at a livery stable.

The various cultural centers and meccas serving the thirsty, hungry and misunderstood that Stump visited for the next few days are no longer, all banned by law in the name of dubious progress. But they furnished Stump Duncan a festiveness unknown on a remote ranch.

After his pockets were nearly depleted, he recovered Willow from the livery stable and headed for the 7UP.

The first night out of Prescott, he arrived at Simmons in Williamson Valley as the first snow of winter began to fall. The storm grew in intensity and soon developed into a genuine blizzard.

Stump was invited to spend the night at the Cross Triangle bunkhouse. After dinner, the snow still falling outside, some of the boys suggested a poker game. While Stump had very little money left, he was a positive thinker and saw in the invitation an opportunity to replenish the pockets he emptied in Prescott.

Late in the afternoon, two days later, Mrs. Hill spotted Stump walking up the road, step by slow step, through the deep snow. He was wet, half-frozen and exhausted. Presuming the poor man had been trapped in the blizzard, she sat him down by the stove, stripped his soaked clothes from him and wrapped his chilled, block-like body in dry blankets. Then she began to thaw him out with hot buttered rum.

Finally, Stump began to talk, but the topics of the town were secondary. First, he related his ordeal in the blizzard and told of losing the old horse in the storm.

"He froze plumb to death," lied Stump, "I done all I could, but the snow and the cold were just too much for the old boy."

The Hills regretted the loss of Willow but were grateful that Stump had survived and was able to reach the ranch.

On a supply trip to Prescott the following spring, the Hills saw old Willow and his new owner in Williamson Valley. They stopped their wagon and had a pleasant visit with the rider, drawing from him, bit by bit, the story of his horse.

When they returned to the ranch several days later, they first unloaded the wagon, then began to question Stump, mentioning they had seen a rider on Willow in Williamson Valley. At first, Stump expressed surprise, suggesting that if it was the same horse, it had revived after being left for dead.

Then he returned to the truth and told them the story of the all-night poker game and the losses he had suffered. The Hills, familiar with the frailties of cowboys, heard his confession with clinical compassion. Stump agreed that when he had saved enough money, he would either buy back Willow or replace him. The matter was dropped.

Some months later, he bought a fine colt from the Dumbbell Ranch and led him to the 7UP. He suggested they name the colt Blizzard.

The Hills named him Poker.

I have thought of him, remembered him and seen him with my eyes closed for the past thirty Christmas seasons. An Arizona institution, he crossed the bridge of multi-culture long before it became a staple in our vocabularies.

The little native stone cottage he called home shone bright in the December sun that morning. His two old dogs of Indian origin uncurled themselves, stood up, stared, scratched, yawned, and sauntered to a sunny spot where the rock wall reflected what little heat there was.

One old Navajo had come to help unload the truck and he, too, waited outside while the Reverend Shine Smith, minister sans pulpit, warmed up last night's coffee and dressed to meet the day. Christmas was a week away.

Shine Smith had come to Indian country several years before, as a well-regarded missionary, sponsored and supported by a national congregation. But each year he spent among the Navajos wrought a shift of his values. Now, with a good Navajo vocabulary and an intimate insight into a culture other than his own, survival ranked with salvation.

Shine, in fact, had come to believe the social needs of the Navajos far exceeded their religious needs. They had, he observed, great spiritual resources. What they lacked was food, clothing, and shelter.

From this concept grew the Shine Smith Christmas Party, held each year on the Navajo Reservation, supported by donations of food, clothing and toys from several Arizona organizations and individuals in virtually every state in the Union.

When I first met Shine, his hair was as full and white as Santa's and his cheeks were wind-blown crimson. He had long before severed his relationship with the church which had sent him on the mission. He had tried to explain to the church officials that giving birth to a baby in a stable was considered a luxury by mothers who had brought forth their babies beneath a bush. Shine and the church departed friends.

Shine Smith continued to work among the Navajo as an individual alone. In those times, before World War II, reservation roads were only ruts and a trip from Tonalea to Lukachukai and return might take a week. Worse yet, it might cost you as much as $20, and no church saw fit to dip into the mission fund to aid a renegade they once called reverend.

Shine built a support system. He came to the attention of a young Phoenix businessman who had a full interest in Indians, a half-interest in a Cessna Skymaster, and an eye on a United States Senate seat. Barry Goldwater spoke to service clubs and wrote letters, asking for support for Shine Smith and his work among the Navajo. Soon Shine was able to live and work on a decent budget and his annual Christmas party grew larger every year.

It was a cold December morning when I last saw him. He invited the old Navajo and me into his house for a cup of hot coffee. The Navajo was going to help unload my truck, filled with gifts of food, clothing and a few toys, sent by a civic group of Prescott. As we three sipped our coffee and listened to the cedar wood pop in Shine's tin stove, the old Indian began to talk.

"We do this every year. We work hard. We get all this stuff. We give it all away at once. In one day we give it all away. We give too much to too many just once a year. Why don't we give a little bit every day? Give a toy or some food or a coat to someone. Give something every day."

Shine looked at me and smiled. "That's not a bad idea, is it?" he asked. "Give a little bit every day. That way every day would be Christmas. Maybe that's the way we should treat each other; give a little bit every day. That's what Christmas is really about. You can learn a lot from these people," Shine said.

Merry Christmas! Give a little bit every day. Merry Christmas! Shine Smith and an old Navajo had the right idea.

In the pre-Depression days of Prescott, Arizona the town was saddled not only with the scourge of prohibition, but the community also suffered a serious shortage of decent ravioli.

Finally, an Italian bootlegger and his mistress solved the problem. Although I knew little of the bootlegging business, I did have an active role in ravioli acquisition.

The woman's name was Mary. Besides being the chief executive officer and madam of an active business, she was a master at making ravioli. Her corporate headquarters was a two-story brick building on the east side of what is now the Prescott Middle School playing field.

The churches took away most of her clientele on Sundays so Mary devoted her day to making wonderful ravioli. When word of Mary's avocation reached my parents' ears, they were delighted. It did, however, present a problem.

Certainly, my father, a prominent citizen, could not be seen going up the steps to Mary's, even for ravioli. For my mother to be seen going in or out of the brick building, would have been out of the question. My sister was five years older than I, so her age and gender eliminated her from fetching our Sunday dinner at Mary's.

This left me, about ten or eleven years old, the blush of innocence on my cheeks and freckles on my youthful nose. On the Sunday evenings when we were to have Mary's ravioli for dinner, my mother would drive me downtown and park in the alley behind the brick building.

I carried a steel tray up the steps and gave it to Mary. After a short wait in an empty hall, Mary would emerge from her living quarters and hand me the tray full of ravioli covered with wax paper. I would then hand her the envelope containing the payment my mother had given me. Mary always admonished me to be careful carrying the tray down the stairs.

This delightful supply of meat ravioli with red sauce lasted until her lover went to prison and she left town.

Through a Depression, three wars and three Republican administrations, I could find no place in my home town to delight my palate with the ground meat, pasta and red sauce. I considered moving.

A dear friend served a good ravioli at the Elks Club on rare occasions. This, and trips to St. Louis or San Francisco, occasionally quenched my passion. In that grim period of my life, I was uneasy, apprehensive and unsatisfied.

There are long-time residents of Prescott who complain about change. Traffic, population density and the loss of a slow-paced life have caused them unhappiness. Not so with me.

As the idyllic little village I was born in grew, with it came the gifts of many Magi. Among these were La Bruzza's Ristorante where raviolis which rival those of days past are available on demand. I am grateful for this community resource.

Sometimes, I still miss Mary's.

Between 1880 and 1930, a principal industry of Arizona centered around health-seekers. They basked in the dry desert sun, in hopes of ridding their racked bodies of the dread disease, tuberculosis. From the thousands of "lungers" who were cured, many remained to become leaders in industry, arts, business and professions.

They came from all parts of the world and all stations of life, and enriched the cultural and technical resources of the state. Their varied backgrounds benefitted a frontier state with a cosmopolitan quality.

One such seeker of health was Frank Holme, a master printer, designer and book publisher. Holme was born in West Virginia in 1868 and began his artistic career as an illustrator. He worked for several newspapers in the days when illustrations rather than photographs were used and he won initial recognition from his detailed drawings of the Johnstown, Pennsylvania Flood.

This led to a job with a Chicago paper where he acquired some printing equipment and formed his own book publishing business, the Bandar Log Press, named for the monkey people in Rudyard Kipling's *Jungle Book*. At age thirty-four, he contracted tuberculosis. He traveled to Phoenix, Arizona Territory, in 1902, in hopes of regaining his health.

As Holme was without funds, a friend sold 100 shares of the Bandar Log Press to his friends at $25 a copy to be paid back in the form of hand-printed books. In the two-year life of the press in Phoenix, six titles were issued in editions of 200 to 600 copies.

All were handcrafted, printed on a hand press; Holme did the illustrations, then carved them on woodblocks.

The University of Arizona Library has a full set of Bandars. The Huntington Library of Pasadena, California, has several of the publications and much of Holme's material. Now regarded as rare, a Bandar Log book is a valuable collector's item.

While in Phoenix, Holme lived on a ranch near the Arizona Canal and what is now Interstate-17. The ranch provided tents to shelter the health-seekers. The press was housed in an abandoned chicken coop. Here, Will Robinson's first book, *Her Navajo Lover* , was crafted. Bandar Log's best known publication, *Poker Rubaiyat,* was a product of this desert enterprise. Most of the books measured eight by ten inches and some illustrations ran to as many as nine separate colors.

While many of the tuberculosis patients of early Arizona regained their health and lived long and productive lives, such was not the happy fate of Frank Holme. Perhaps because of his constant drive and unceasing self demands, he died in Denver in 1904, following a massive pulmonary hemorrhage. The Bandar Log Press died with him; but out of that desert chicken coop at the beginning of the century came some of the finest work of the bookman's art.

Billy Bob's Texas is not your average watering spot. Located in Fort Worth, it is done in Texas scale — three separate restaurants, all types of entertainment and the biggest bar in the Lone Star State. The Fort Worth Fire Department permits only 5,500 customers at a time; 6,000 might crowd things a bit.

Owner Billy Bob Barnett also is scaled to the Lone Star State. Billy Bob stands, six feet, five inches. He elbows his way across a room like an NBA forward in a regional playoff. If he dropped ten years and twenty pounds, he could take on the front four of the Dallas Cowboys at any parking lot in Texas.

Billy Bob is sort of a Texas Historical Site. He's the closest thing to Vesuvius there is in Texas and his social demeanor is somewhat similar. One August Billy Bob played a pivotal role in a bottle-throwing fracas in a Dallas nightclub. Some misunderstanding had developed, but the scope of the conflict did not require the intervention of the Dallas Police Department. The removal of Billy Bob from the premises was an in-house operation.

His finest hour in outrageous character development occurred several years ago when he won an impressive wager by eating a dead rodent and washing it down with a bottle of beer. Billy Bob to this day denies he ate a dead rat and drank a bottle of Miller Lite. He modestly declares it was a mouse and a Schlitz.

His most recent social indiscretion happened on a Labor Day weekend when the Mayor of Saginaw, Michigan was visiting Saginaw, Texas, a suburb of Fort Worth. Room 111 at the Sandpiper Inn had been reserved for His Honor from Michigan. When the manager of the inn noticed several orders of drinks and hors d'oeuvres being delivered to room 111 before Hizzonor had arrived, police were called.

About this time, the Michigan mayor showed up and accompanied the police to his room. When the police knocked on the door, it was opened by a young lady clad in a rather inadequate towel. In the room's Jacuzzi they found Billy Bob with yet another young lady, not nearly as well dressed as the first one.

The mayor from Michigan, unaware that such amenities are not uncommon in Texas, denied that he knew the frolicking trio. Billy Bob, with grandeur and panache, apologized for the unfortunate incident and, with his Jacuzzi den mothers, left the premises.

When on the way to his car he was informed he had disturbed the mayor of Saginaw, Michigan, he resolved to make amends. He returned to the room with a case of liquor, a gift for Hizzonor. Unfortunately, while still chatting with the mayor in the finest Texas tradition, Billy Bob was informed that one of his female friends had been placed under arrest.

Billy Bob blew up. His first move was to pick up the case of liquor which had been his peace offering and throw it across the once well ordered room. The noise of the shattering glass wasn't so bad, but the wanton waste of the contents of the bottles unnerved all present. When Billy Bob witnessed the whiskey being absorbed by the shag carpet, something broke inside him.

By the time the Fort Worth police managed to subdue him, the mayor's room looked like Hitler's bunker the day after the Russians came to town. Billy Bob spent Labor Day, our national holiday, in the Fort Worth jail because of what the police regarded as anti-social conduct.

The following day, the charge was reduced to public intoxication and Billy Bob was released on a $56 bond. My friends inform me that since the Labor Day Jacuzzi Jubilee, Billy Bob's demeanor has been exemplary, not unlike that of an Eton scholar.

Billy Bob is a good ol' boy. He just can't handle Jacuzzis.

During March of 1883 a well-dressed middle-aged gentleman named James Addison Reavis casually entered the office of Surveyor General J.W. Robbins in Tucson, Arizona and filed a plethora of impressive-looking documents to prove his claim to the then unknown but fabulous Peralta Grant.

Reavis, who from that day forward would be known as the Baron of Arizona, was no small time land grabber. This ex-Confederate soldier and Missouri streetcar conductor had, with that simple gesture, laid claim to an area which ran seventy-five miles wide from near Silver City, New Mexico, west to a line just beyond Phoenix, Arizona. Within the bounds of his fraudulent barony were the Arizona towns of Tempe, Mesa, Clifton, Globe, Casa Grande and Florence.

The Southern Pacific Railroad crossed a corner of his claim and many rich mines, including the Silver King, removed riches from his fabricated domain. Reavis had done his research. He was well aware that under the Treaty of Guadalupe Hidalgo of 1848, which concluded the Mexican War, and also by the terms of the Gadsden Purchase in 1854, the United States was compelled to recognize the validity of previous land grants by the Spanish and Mexican governments.

Reavis had first come to Arizona in 1879 as a subscription agent for the *San Francisco Examiner.* He was intelligent enough to see the great potential of vast areas of virgin land. He had developed a talent for forgery. The two factors converged in swindle. He went to work adding to, altering, removing and inserting forgeries in the official title depositories of Spain and Mexico.

The human connection Reavis chose was one of equal cunning. He fabricated a family lineage beginning with one Don Nemecio de Peralta de la Córdoba. Reavis explained that Peralta had been given the title of Baron de los Colorados by His Majesty King Ferdinand VI of Spain in 1748. With this, the generous Ferdinand also bestowed a modest grant of some twelve million acres, the Peralta Grant, of course, located in the new territory of Arizona, a dry and rock-worn desert. Reavis told how he had purchased the title to the grant from one George Willing, a ne'er-do-well miner who had drifted in and out of Arizona since 1864.

The line of lies continued: Willing had purchased the title from a member of the Peralta family, one Miguel

Peralta, a sick and poverty-ridden citizen of Sonora, Mexico, who had taken his paltry pay and returned to his native state to die in a degree of comfort. Reavis said Willing then recorded the deed in the Yavapai County Courthouse in March 1874. Willing died the following day, on the banks of Granite Creek. The cause? "Exposure and privation." The *Weekly Arizona Miner* suggested on March 20, 1874 that the death of one George Willing occurred under strange and unwitnessed circumstances. No record was ever found to prove the birth, life or death of a Miguel Peralta.

The last link in Reavis' chain of claim was perhaps his strongest. From Sonora, he brought to California a very young orphan girl, dainty, demure and classically structured. There he had her privately educated. He forged a record of her birth and placed it into the records of a California parish. The document showed her to be the last surviving descendant of the Peralta family. He then bestowed upon this unsuspecting child the title of Baroness of Arizona, convinced her of this identity and married her.

After this rather elaborate marriage had been duly recorded, James Addison Reavis invaded Arizona.

Confusion and anxiety generated by the claim of James Addison Reavis lasted for about twelve years. The huge Peralta Grant was regarded as a malignant flaw on thousands of deeds and titles. Lawyers of national repute examined the Reavis documents and pronounced them sound, and unassailable in any court.

But there were skeptics too. Shortly after Reavis had filed his original claim, Surveyor General Robbins died of tuberculosis. He was succeeded by the hard-nosed Royal Johnson, also a talented attorney. Johnson's term in office was interrupted by a change of national administration, but he never ceased to pore through records for a clue to refute the claim. He built his case, sometimes at great personal expense.

Thomas Weedin, the editor of the *Florence Enterprise,* fanned the flames with newsprint which he hoped would consume the fraud. When the Florence School Board paid Reavis for a quit claim deed to school property, Weedin branded the transaction as blackmail. Another editor, Homer H. McNeil, of the *Arizona Gazette,* also urged people to resist the swindle by refusing to recognize the claim of Reavis. He lost much of his effectiveness, however, when it became known that he had paid Reavis for a deed to his own property and had it recorded. Other individuals and companies also chose to play safe and render unto Reavis the tribute necessary to purchase their security and swell his bulging pockets. The Southern Pacific Railroad coughed up $50,000 and the Silver King Mine sent the Baron $25,000.

Reavis could do no wrong. As a symbol of success, his lovely young bride Carmelita presented him with handsome twin boys. In high silk hat and a frock coat, his royal feet cradled in the fine black boots of a gentleman, the Baron of Arizona roamed his empire and beyond. Wherever he went — Madrid, London or New York — he collected documents to reinforce his claim. He cultivated men of prestige and influence. He dressed his sons in velvet and lace. His ivory-skinned bride wore only the original creations of Old World origin. Travel was always by first class train or ocean steamer and the premier hotels of the world were grateful for his flamboyant patronage.

By 1889 several cracks began to appear in the Baron's empire. A watermark on some of the documents was traced to a Wisconsin paper manufacturer. Poor Spanish grammar flawed other papers submitted by Reavis. A printer in Florence named Stammering Bill recognized a typeface as a special kind from a typefounder's house in San Francisco. The royal reign of Reavis was coming to an end.

On July 17, 1896, James Addison Reavis was ordered by a federal judge in Sante Fe, New Mexico, to pay a $5,000 fine and serve two years. He was released from prison on April 18, 1898. Carmelita was living in a Denver flat barely supporting herself and twin sons as a milliner.

The fabric of fraud had by now become a fact in the mind of James A. Reavis. He roamed the streets of Denver, San Francisco and Phoenix in his tattered suits of yesterday. When he was confined in the Los Angeles County Poor House a loyal friend gave him the money to visit his divorced wife and the boys in Denver. There, in a modest apartment on Larimer Square, he died November 20, 1914, age seventy-one.

James Addison Reavis proved to be a mortal man. But the Baron of Arizona? Ah! That's quite a different proposition.

The only thing that can match the color of Arizona's cliffs and canyons are its characters. These sandpainted people usually end up in politics or prison, often more qualified for the latter. There were exceptions. John B. Allen was one of those prismatic personalities who managed to live within the harsh law of a raw frontier.

Allen's pre-Arizona life is obscure. This is not uncommon. Numerous individuals in and out of public life still come to Arizona to close the door of the past and open one of the future. Allen was thirty-nine years of age and destitute when he arrived in Yuma in 1857.

When the gold fever hit the lower Gila River, and Gila City was created out of tents and wikiups, Allen was among the many who tried to get rich with a pick and pan. He failed.

He headed east to Calabazas, Tubac, Tombstone and finally, Tucson in Southern Arizona. Here, in a primitive desert town he saw a need for some joy of yesterday to brighten the bleak land. Allen was a superb baker and he used this gift to supply dried apple pies to soldiers, miners, merchants, gamblers and wanton women. Business boomed. He charged a dollar a pie. His product was superior, and apple pie, then as now, seemed to symbolize what was right with the country.

The happy news of Allen and his pies spread rapidly all over the territory. As Americans are wont to do, they rechristened John B. Allen. He became known as Pie Allen and his product was as well regarded as twelve straight passes at the crap table.

Pie purchased 160 acres at Maricopa Wells where he grew alfalfa hay and opened the only store on the stage line between Tucson and Yuma. His ranching and farming activities expanded rapidly and he opened additional mercantile businesses in Tubac and Tucson.

When the silver boom hit Tombstone, Pie Allen built the finest store in the territory to meet the needs of the people. He became a wealthy man. Defeated by the pan, he prospered by the pie.

Pie Allen was soon elected to the Territorial Legislature. He is not remembered fondly in Prescott for it was Pie Allen who orchestrated the move of the territorial capital from Prescott to Tucson in 1867.

He became territorial treasurer and eliminated deficits. In the mid 1870s he was appointed adjutant general of the territory and became known as General Pie. Tucson twice elected him mayor. He had prisoners work all night sweeping the packed adobe streets. They first wetted them down, then smoothed them with long prison-made mesquite brooms.

In April, 1899, Pie Allen at 81 years of age was suffering from terminal cancer. The citizens of Tucson chose to honor him with perhaps the strangest testimonial dinner ever held in Arizona.

There had been some difference of opinion on what kind of gift they would present him with. In an effort to be helpful, Zeckendorf and Company offered to supply the gift, something useful to him for years to come. They knew that an old man who had spent more than half of his life on an unsettled frontier would have no illusions about his own mortality.

The dinner enjoyed and the dessert (apple pie) consumed, a few speeches followed. Then his friends presented Allen with a handsome tombstone which he gratefully accepted. Knowing that death was but days away, the inscription read:

"John B. Allen
Born 1818 — Died 1899
Territorial Treasurer six years
Mayor of Tucson two terms
A man without an enemy."

The black horse came on time for Pie Allen.

Eastward from the Harquahalas,
At a place called Cactus Flat,
Lived and toiled an old prospector
Just a gray old desert rat.

He loved the desert, but his was a cautious love, never confusing beauty with safety. Ned White knew that for every bloom there were ten thousand thorns, and what was left of a lifetime was carried in a canteen.

White was born at Fort Russell, on the outskirts of Cheyenne, Wyoming, in 1873. His father was an Irish immigrant who had made the U.S. Army his career. Upon retirement he brought his family to Arizona Territory to take up a homestead.

When young Ned first heard the tales of instant riches being plucked from quartz outcroppings, or sifted from sand and water in a rocker box, he became a miner.

But Ned White is not remembered as a miner in spite of his thousand sorties into the desert and mountains. He is, however, immortalized as "the bard of Brewery Gulch" and "the miner's poet."

Ned grew up on the desert near Fort McDowell and from there wandered into every active mining district in central and southern Arizona. Like most, he never struck it rich, but he observed and reported a type of life long gone from the Southwest scene. Tombstone, Wickenburg, Weaver and Texas Canyon were all open classrooms for Ned White.

Before he went to work for Phelps Dodge in Bisbee, he had roamed from the Chocolate Mountains to the Chiricahuas and from the Bradshaws to the Sierra Madres.

Ned wrote a weekly column for the *Brewery Gulch Gazette* for many years and published poems in various other journals. When he retired from Phelps Dodge, he would sit on the grassy plaza at the foot of Brewery Gulch in Bisbee and visit with the retired and offshift miners. The Cousin Jacks, the Finns, Slavs and the Matador Miners from Mexico all knew and loved him. He too, knew their customs, and could communicate in their mother tongues.

If there ever was a man who should be remembered for saving some of what was, it is Ned White. He was more than a miner's poet, he was a miner's saint. He said of them:

May they live long in my memory,
Around the ashes of my camp,
'Mid the foothills of the Bradshaws
Down along the Hassayamp.

While researching Arizona sheriffs, I ran across the almost forgotten name of Pete Gabriel. Pete was not a "cowboy" sheriff, but a miner. He lacked charisma and quips of that flamboyant fraternity which included Commodore Perry Owens, Buckey O'Neill and Lon Jordan. Jordan bridged an era from mounted posses to law enforcement aircraft.

Pete Gabriel was an Alsatian by birth. Both his parents died crossing the desert on the way to California. Pete was just six years old at the time and a series of desert dwellers fed, clothed and housed Pete until he reached sixteen. He worked for several prospectors to earn his keep and learn the geology of the gold-seeker.

Bright, well-liked and seduced by the ghost of gold, he soon went his own way to dry desert camps where he had little luck. When the office of sheriff of Pinal County offered an alternative, Pete ran for it and was elected in the early 1880s.

For a few years, Sheriff Pete Gabriel kept what little peace there was in Pinal County. The tiny town of Florence was but a dot on a dusty desert, as yet without the commerce a state prison later would bring. Discharging the duties of his office well, but still devoted to his mining claims, Pete decided not to run again.

One of his deputies, Joe Phy, eagerly announced his intention to succeed Gabriel. Phy, alas, packed some political baggage. His age far exceeded his IQ and on more than one occasion he had mistreated prisoners. One of these sadistic beatings nearly resulted in death. When Phy asked Gabriel to support him, he declined to do so. In due time, Phy was defeated and Pete Gabriel returned to his mining claims. Phy was openly bitter.

In late May, 1888, Pete Gabriel rode into Florence, put his horse in the livery stable and retired to the cool comfort of the Tunnel Saloon to play a little poker. The afternoon passed with the quick pace that poker provides. Soon the saloon lamps were lighted as dusk faded. As in all short and violent confrontations, accounts of what happened next differed. One thing was certain; everyone seemed to see him at once.

Joe Phy stood in the doorway, revolver in one hand, hunting knife in the other. Without a word, Phy pointed his revolver at Pete and fired. The bullet hit Pete in the chest and knocked him to the floor. Automatically, Pete drew his pistol and sent a shot through Phy's midsection. Phy kept coming. Gabriel was hit again, this time in the right hip. Gabriel emptied his revolver into the crazed man as he advanced. Finally, Phy slumped to the floor like an empty gunnysack. It was over. The fodder of fiction.

Pete Gabriel was exonerated of any wrongdoing and remained in Florence until he recovered from his wounds. When he regained his health he returned to his claims in the Pioneer Mining District. Here, with typical Alsatian tenacity, he built a cabin. Pete lived a long but spartan life, alone, aloof. Had it not been for that violent event on a warm May evening in 1888, Sheriff Pete Gabriel might have slipped through the screen of Arizona history.

The OK Corral was history when he came to Tombstone. Tombstone, however, was far from being tame. Con men, hardrock miners and cowboys cruised the wide-open town; all sustained the reputation the community had honestly won.

The young Episcopal priest, Endicott Peabody,

arrived in Tombstone following his graduation from Cheltenham College in England and the Episcopal Theological Seminary at Cambridge, Massachusetts. He was aware that his stay would be short, for he planned to return to New England to establish a school. He had agreed to serve an interim period in Tombstone. Being young and adventurous, he looked forward to the unique experience.

Peabody was a big man, a little over 200 pounds, standing six-foot-two. Born in Salem, Massachusetts, he was fond of boxing and baseball, and was a student of the French novelist Balzac. A knowledge of Balzac had a limited use in Tombstone, but boxing and baseball proved invaluable in his new relationships.

He pulled no punches in either the ring or the pulpit.

While he frequented the saloons and gambling halls pursuing his pastoral duties, he often stood in the pulpit on Sundays and preached the evils of such an environment. On one occasion he delivered a steaming sermon on cattle rustling (thou shall not covet thy neighbor's cow) to which an advocate of the art took sour exception.

The individual who thought he had been personally cited in the cattle rustling sermon began to confront and harass him. Peabody would attempt to reason and assure him, but the man stepped up his threats. To resolve the conflict short of a second OK Corral, Reverend Peabody suggested a boxing match in a local bar. Tickets would be sold to benefit Tombstone's less fortunate. The ruffian, clamoring at a chance to clobber the clergy, accepted.

It was no match. Peabody countered with nothing but defensive jabs until his opponent threw his Sunday punch which never landed. The reverend's punch was even more potent than his sermon and was backed by two hundred pounds of well-coordinated clergyman.

There endeth the epistle.

The boxing victory did much to endear Endicott to the community. Although his tenure in the "Town Too Tough To Die" was only six months, he became an atypical legend.

When he left Tombstone he went to Groton, Massachusetts, where he founded the Groton School for Boys and served as headmaster. He remained in this capacity from 1884, until his retirement in 1940. In that fifty-six year period he received numerous honors and honorary degrees. Groton was his life and he demanded intellectual, physical and oral excellence of all the young men in his charge. A charming young lad named Franklin Delano Roosevelt was one of his prime products.

Endicott Peabody never returned to Tombstone.

He retired and remained in his home at Groton. The old man slipped into his final sleep in 1944, while sitting in his library chair, a well-worn book in his hand.

Perhaps, as a last flame flickered, he wandered back to Tombstone and heard the dim roar of an approving crowd in a sand-weathered bar on the desert.

CHAPTER

A Ruff Attempt At Humor

Among other prestigious American institutions, the National Liars Club has gone the way of boccie ball, bawdy houses and the Arizona Legislature. At one time the Liars Club held an annual contest and the craftsmanship that was evident among the contestants was magnificent. What once was an art form has in recent years become crude and noncreative. Most of the practicing liars today are tentative. They lack boldness and innovation. In the past two decades, the genuinely gifted liars have become stock brokers or editorial writers. A few of the lower echelon either went to Congress or became pit bosses in Las Vegas. The inept are television commentators.

Arizona has been blessed with some of the finest prevaricators the country has produced. Several have served as governors. Captain John Hance, who arrived at the South Rim of the Grand Canyon in 1881, was one of our best, but he never got into politics. Hance claimed he walked from the South Rim to the North Rim one day when the Canyon was filled to the brim with a cloud bank. He admitted he had used snow shoes on the way over but he had packed the trail so well that coming back to the South Rim, he carried the snow shoes on his back.

His Title, "Captain" was not a rank of mendacity.

In 1906, Arizona was honored with the National Liars Club award, the first prize to Non-Assessable Smith of Yuma County. Smith told of his adventures in the Kofa Mountains while prospecting with his partner, Bill Bolger. He and Bolger had run out of grub and were hungry. It was August and very hot, when Smith decided to go into Yuma for supplies. Bolger remained in camp. After the second day, Bill was near starvation. He began to frantically search the surrounding desert for something to eat. He soon found some Gila Monster eggs but he had no way to cook them. Desperate, he dropped one lizard egg on a flat rock near camp and in no time the egg began to quiver and bubble from the heat. Delighted, Bolger added more eggs and the end result was an appealing omelette.

Three days later Non-Assessable Smith returned to camp and found his partner, Bill, delirious. He put poor Bill in their wagon and headed for Yuma, but Bill staked his final claim soon after Smith got him to the doctor. The undertaker tried to put Bill in the coffin, but he and his helper couldn't begin to lift him. They were amazed to discover that he weighed almost 1,800 pounds. The doctor said he seemed to be ossified. Some strange chemical reaction had taken place.

Apparently the Gila Monster eggs were loaded with cyanide and the rock they were cooked on was gold-bearing. The cyanide had drawn the rich ore and Bill had become a gold-producing cyanide plant. Previously not inclined to do so, Non-Assessable Smith now claimed the body and retired to California, somewhere near Needles.

The new method of gold extraction started a run on Gila Monster eggs, and they have been extremely rare ever since. Non-Assessable Smith told the press that from the day he claimed Bill's body, he had been on Easy Street and had never done a day's work since. There may have been some truth in that.

No question where I could find him. He's in the same spot every year. He puts his aluminum chair almost in the middle of the street, brings a cooler full of cold drinks and watches the parade. I wormed my way up close to him.

"Stanley, how are you? Has the parade come up to your expectations?"

"Well, yes and no. I guess I sound like a politician, don't I?"

"Maybe you should be one."

"That reminds me. Do you remember a few years ago you told me the Utah Legislature had a bill that would require anybody who ran for public office to have a license."

"Oh yes." I said. "I remember it well. However, the bill was defeated."

"The basic idea is sound."

"I have to agree with you, Stanley."

"As I see it, you have to have a license to get married, own a dog, drive a car, go hunting or open a savings and loan. All those things frequently end in disaster, so a license to run for office sounds like a good idea."

"But, Stanley, what if an individual couldn't afford the license, or had some moral objection to it?"

"Well, look at Jesse Jackson, he ain't no lottery winner but he flies all over the country givin' speeches. I think he just gets a kick out of traveling and the

Republican National Committee pays his expenses. Every time he goes on television the Republicans get closer to a landslide."

"You may be right, Stanley."

"Why didn't the Utah license bill pass?"

"It was amended to death. It became unrealistic. The amendments required the candidate for office to meet certain standards. One amendment said that the candidate had to be able to read twenty-five words per minute, then another amendment raised that to fifty. The law required the candidate to have an IQ of sixty-eight or better. The standards were just too high."

"Well, anyway, Utah had a good idea. Maybe we could get our Legislature to pass it next session. Utah has given us a lot: the best skiing in North America, great hunting and fishing, beautiful scenery and the Mormon Tabernacle Choir."

"Stanley, did you ever hear of Norman Douglas?"

"Yeah, I think so. Wasn't he a Supreme Court justice?"

"That was a different Douglas, Stanley. William O. Douglas. He was both colorful and controversial but created more controversy than color. Norman Douglas was a writer."

"Well, it must be nice to have a job that you don't have to use either mind or muscle."

"Now, Stanley. Anyway, Norman Douglas said: 'To find a friend we must close one eye... to keep him, two.'"

"Well, did you ever hear of Yogi Berra?"

"I sure have, Stanley. One of our great twentieth century philosophers."

"He should be the commissioner of baseball. Do you know what he said?"

"Tell me."

"Well, Yogi said, when his team was losing and the

stands were empty, 'If people don't want to come out to the ballpark, nobody's going to stop them.'"

"Here comes the end of the parade, Stanley."

"Well, help me carry this ice chest back to my pickup."

The house no longer stands. Some scant evidence of its rock foundation is still there and a few small walnut trees pierce what once was its floor.

Seventy-five years ago this real Arizona ranch home was a long way from the town of Prescott, now a thirty-minute drive. The ranch was ably operated by the father, a hard working mother, two bright daughters and an adventuresome little boy. While the daughters helped their mother around the house little Clarence was permitted to go with his father and the men. He helped with the cattle and horses, checked on the windmills, put out salt, and, at six years of age, was a rapidly developing cowboy.

Alas, when he was six years old, his mother died. After ward, his father's unmarried sister came to live with them. She taught the girls the arts of a ranch household, but little Clarence still worked with his father and the cowboys. The frustrations inherent in handling cattle lead to language not acceptable to maiden aunts. Clarence, of course, by working with the cowboys, had added a few colorful expressions to his juvenile vocabulary.

But, on the first Christmas his aunt was the woman of the house, he was still an ardent believer in Santa Claus. On Christmas Eve he hung his stocking as he always had on the large stone fireplace in the living room. It was in this stocking that he expected Santa to place his Christmas presents. His mother had always seen that this was done. After the children had gone to bed his aunt arranged the childrens' gifts around the tree. Then as an added surprise she filled little Clarence's stocking with nuts and hard candy. The fireplace still flickered a lazy flame when little Clarence sneaked down the stairway very early Christmas morning.

Before anyone was up, little Clarence wanted to feel his Christmas stocking hanging on the fireplace in the darkened room. From the shape of what the stocking contained, he knew he could tell what Santa Claus had brought him. His little hands could detect nothing in the stocking but small round lumps.

It was then he became a cowboy again and expressed his disappointment in Santa Claus, when he muttered under his breath:

"Marbles. Nothin' but marbles. God damn his old soul!"

Next to television game programs, murder trials and restroom poetry, polls are the favorite entertainment of Americans. Election years are fraught with various polls. Not just the ranking of the candidate for office, but even the regional popularity of movies, music or martinis.

One of the most influential newspapers in the country, the *Des Moines Register*, recently conducted a lifestyle poll to determine the taste and trends of its readership.

The poll exploded some myths and converted others to reality. For example, I, along with thousands, believed bib overalls were the exclusive uniform of farmers. Not so. In Iowa, thirty percent of the entire population own a pair of the bibs.

Farmers of course, are among those counted, but young ladies and BMW Yuppies are donning Big Mac bibs for Sunday brunch at the University Club.

Ralph Lauren has not entered the field but a polo player logo on the left hand side of the bib is a cinch to be here by Christmas.

These Iowa bib boomers revealed other strange leanings in the *Register's* poll. Twenty four percent of those polled use ornaments on their lawns, and believe there is life on other planets.

Now that another issue of Prescott Frontier Days is over (known to many locals as Geek Week), I decided to conduct my own public opinion poll regarding Prescott lifestyle, taste and trends. the margin of error has been determined at seventy percent plus or minus.

A cross section of the community was interviewed: an alternative lifestyle beekeeper, a Prescott College student doing independent studies on his GED, and an animal rights activist who is now on a sabbatical.

The results were astounding! An incredible ninety-seven percent of Prescott citizens own one or more pairs of Levi's. The bad news is only eleven percent can button the top button.

Happily, only eight percent of Prescott lawns have pink flamingos, frogs or plastic chipmunks in residence. However, one high roller in Wildwood has a teak garden bench on his/her lawn with "In your heart you know he's right" carved on the back.

If everyone was telling the truth, Prescott has virtually no AIDS problem which proves we are doing something right. (That was rather poorly worded.)

My poll disclosed what many of us have long suspected. Prescott is the wheelchair license plate capital of the country. Anything from acne to prefrontal lobotomy will increase your odds for getting a handicap parking space.

The vast majority of the male population of Prescott over forty years of age suffers midlife crisis. The good news is that seventeen percent of them are in remission.

I'm one of the lucky ones.

The name of the town really isn't that important. Throughout the West there were hundreds of little towns with similar, small, one-man saddle shops located in these communities, which owed their lives to the cash converted from cattle. This saddle shop was on one of the side streets within staggering distance of some of the best bars in town. It was obvious that the old saddle maker had given some thought to the location when he opened his shop. A student of cowboys, he was well aware that a visit to the bar was the first priority of the breed after weeks on a dry and dusty range. There were other advantages too; three or four shots of red-eye caused many a cowboy to overestimate his personal resources. With a cowboy, whiskey seemed to be the elixir of impulse buying.

It was not unusual then, for the old saddle maker to feel the little frame building shake in periods close to payday, as an uncoordinated body hit the oak door before his thumb had depressed the release latch.

Adjoining the door of such establishments was a plate glass window with gold leaf lettering on it which proudly proclaimed the name of the firm and the quality of workmanship which occurred behind the portals. Some convenience merchandise was carried on the bare board shelves of such establishments. Things like currycombs, saddle blankets and manila rope. The principal pursuit of the proprietor, however, was leatherwork. The boots and saddles he so carefully crafted were expressions of the artistic temperament of both the maker and the purchaser. The shop was stacked with various types and grades of leather and the scents they released puffed many nostrils with a preconceived pride of ownership.

The saddles the old man made were cut, fitted and tooled, then formed to the type of saddle tree the customer specified. The tree itself was made from the wood of the American Elm. The extent of the decoration of such saddles was frequently determined by the purchaser's individual economic situation and ego, and the handmade boots were generally ordered on the same basis.

On this winter afternoon it was quiet in the little shop and the smell of the tanned leather was intensified by the heat of the old iron stove. He came through the door on the second try, dressed in a sheepskin jacket, sweat-stained Stetson and Levi's long overdue at the laundry. His sagebrush sabbatical spent at a local saloon had convinced him of the need for a new pair of boots. He leaned against the crude wooden counter, but the old man behind it barely nodded an acknowledgment of his presence; he came not from the school of Dale Carnegie merchandising. Ignoring the absence of amenities the cowboy began to tell the old craftsman what he wanted.

"I need a new pair of work boots. I ain't no dude with a wad I can't wrap both hands around so I don't want nothin' fancy. I want a pair of plain old work boots, black oiled leather with maybe a regular three row stitch done with ordinary orange thread. Nothin' fancy, you understand. I'm just a cowboy workin' for wages and I don't want none of them fancy dude boots with all kinds of colored leather on 'em making a picture of a chipmunk tryin' to screw a butterfly."

The old man knew just what he wanted.

This doesn't mean anything to anyone but me, but today is my birthday and the frequency and magnitude of that depressing event makes me aware of some changes.

I have never known anyone who wasn't conscious of the passing of time. Nevertheless several How To Tell When Your Growing Older Lists have been published, rewritten, compiled and modified.

To observe my natal day, I have invented a new list. It contains some golden oldies and I have added a few new entries. If you can relate to the following you will know what is happening.

If you cannot relate to it, save it. It's only a matter of time.

•••

Your friends all die young,
but your enemies seem to be immortal.

•••

Almost everything hurts;
what doesn't hurt, doesn't work.

•••

The gleam in your eyes
is caused by glaucoma medication.

•••

You feel like the morning after the night before,
and you went to bed right after the evening news.

•••

All the names in your little black book end with an M.D.

•••

You get winded touch-toning a long distance call.

•••

When you fill the birdbath it distends your bladder.

•••

Your children all look middle-aged.

•••

No one returns your phone calls but a mortician.

•••

You want to buy an ultra suede coat;
the clerk suggests buckskins.

•••

Your three martini lunch is now Meals on Wheels.

•••

You can't stand people who are intolerant.

•••

You interrupt your own conversations.

•••

You believe in a hereafter
but would rather go to Wrigley Field.

•••

Your knees buckle, but your belt won't.

•••

You sink your teeth into a T-bone and they stay there.

•••

Your dining room is too big
and your medicine cabinet too small.

•••

You join a health club and forget where it's located.

•••

Wearing your sheepskin ear muffs is the most sensual experience you have had since V-J Day.

•••

Your back goes out more than you do.

•••

You list all your appointments for the next six months, but can't find the book.

•••

Your girlfriend is on the pill... Tylenol.

Probably it comes as no surprise that I don't have much faith in psychologists. Normally, I view them with the same absence of adoration as members of Congress.

However, the other day, a psychologist from a small college in the Midwest offered a suggestion I agree with. She advocated that we no longer decorate with mistletoe at Christmas time as it invariably encourages sexual harassment.

I know from personal experience that she is correct. On several occasions when I was in strange surroundings, unaware of the presence of mistletoe, I was assaulted by some seductive, future-centerfold using the Christmas tradition as a ploy to attack me.

I, for one, would enjoy the season more if I was certain I could get through the holidays unsullied.

While banning mistletoe is a good start, many other Christmas traditions are long overdue to be updated or abandoned. I have noticed Santa Claus is wearing the same moth-eaten, red and white suit and his snow-white beard is matted and unsanitary.

The suit is totally inappropriate for descending chimneys. A camouflage jump suit would be better. Perhaps the best move of all — privatize the old boy and contract UPS to deliver all the gifts on Christmas Eve. He could just honk the horn, place the presents under the porchlight and get the hell out of there. You won't find those UPS people coming down the chimney or sitting around drinking milk and eating cookies.

They have ground to cover!

Santa's reindeer are also getting old and becoming problems. Last year, Santa left them on my roof, as usual, while he came down the chimney to place the presents around the tree. You guessed it! It took me a week to clean out the roof gutters and unclog my downspouts. With all those reindeer romping around on the roof, you are going to have trouble.

Sooner or later, Santa will to be in deep yogurt with the feds. As you know, Washington is fanatical about equal opportunity policy. Take a good look at Santa's elves — lily white! If Santa were a coach in the NFL, he would have been long gone by now.

It is common knowledge around the North Pole that the Clauses are not hitting it off too well these days. Mrs. Claus has had it up to here, living in such a harsh climate 365 days a year. Rumor has it that she has served Santa notice that they move the operation to Miami or Palm Springs by next year or she intends to split the blanket. You can hardly blame her — no hairdressers, bridge club or Jazzercise.

While I think of it, we could use some new Christmas Music. Singing chipmunks and the children's choirs do wear a little thin. No self-respecting chipmunk sounds that squeaky and the little kids don't enunciate any better than the local radio announcers.

With the AIDS scare *The Dance of the Sugar Plum Fairies* has been banned in Boston and San Francisco. Next year, I think I will just skip Christmas and have a happy Hanukkah.

There are all kinds of bad guys out there. I am not talking about the Iraqis, Arab terrorists or IRS agents. I mean those fellows called researchers. They don't wear black hats or carry guns but they often have full beards or droopy mustaches and constantly rob the federal treasury. They call it getting a grant.

With the zeal of a television preacher they condemned caffeine, nicotine and alcohol. Their research "proved" these things would kill you. Then some other fellow robbed the federal treasury and did a little research. His study showed that caffeine did no harm. It may, in fact, be of great benefit to the function and performance of the human body. No news yet about nicotine and alcohol, but it's only a matter of time before some researcher will announce that they will make you smart, witty and irresistible.

A year or so ago, a researcher announced that his study showed that a low cholesterol diet greatly reduced your chances for a heart attack. He did point out however, that such a diet may well create impulsive homicidal behavior. Personally I think he is mixed up. When I stopped smoking, I developed impulsive homicidal behavior, and there are still some bozos out there that I would like to take a club to.

A California researcher says that exercise is great for the heart and reduction of body fat *but* it might cause kidney problems and cancer. A New Jersey researcher says seat belts will save your life *but* may bring on sterility. Now he tells me.

Now comes another study from another bandit using taxpayers' money. This one is based at the University Medical Center at Omaha. It is obvious that this sadist intends to destroy civilization as we know it. He may be a Russian spy. He makes the outrageous claim that green and red chile is carcinogenic. This man is un-American. At least he is un-Mexican American.

What do they know in Omaha about chile anyway? Even if this study had been done in Taos, Tucson or Ajo it still would be as tough to swallow as Jonah in the belly of a whale. I would advise those subversives in Omaha to stay in their own backyard and research only corn on the cob and okra.

I have devoted my life to an intensive study of red and green chile and paid for my research out of my own pocket, with a little help from my friends. My great body of chile information proves conclusively that chile (green in particular) is a great boon to humankind second only to penicillin and charge cards.

That oaf in Omaha did say that you'd have to eat at least two pounds of chile a day for it to cause cancer. Just to be sure I am going to play it safe and cut my chile intake down to about one and a half pounds a day. I know it's a sacrifice, but it's for my own good.

As dependent as I am on life support systems, I spend too much time and money at the supermarkets. In all these rialtos I know the location of every critical item such as salsa and foot powder. The secondary supplies, bread, vegetables, caviar and pigs feet, I seldom have any need for, yet I remember their location, as if it were an open bar at the office Christmas party.

Food markets have changed a lot in recent years. They have banks and post offices, and sell prescription drugs, insurance, mutual funds and tombstones. Any day now I expect to see a law office right between the Kitty Litter and ski masks and across the aisle from the eye shades and sleeve garters.

As much time as I spend in food stores, I decided I had better expand my horizons and visit other kinds of emporiums. Whiskey Row (officially Montezuma Street in Prescott, Arizona), once was a continuous block of free standing sanctuaries where one could retreat to reflect on the meaning of life. Now, with rare exception, Montezuma is a string of rubber tomahawk stores and foofoo shops. Few of the venerable centers of arts and science remain. I once knew an oldtimer who detected this trend very early. He swore that if and when anyone on Whiskey Row began selling women's underwear, he would fold his tent and leave town. They did. He did.

Since Prescott has an adequate supply of antique stores I decided to tour a few just to see what was still available from the dim and distant past. My socks are older than most of the antiques in those stores. They price a garlic press as if it were a piece of the True Cross. Elvis Presley had gone to that great gig in the sky before most of this stuff they call antiques was invented.

A close second to the antique stores are the auto part shops. By my count there are about five of these parts places for every auto sales agency. That tells us something about how well put together the modern automobile is. To keep all these parts places busy and prosperous parts must be falling off Detroit's finest like autumn leaves.

I can't get excited about the health food stores. There is always the danger that organic food can become much too organic. Also, I don't consider sunflower seeds and juniper berries fit food except for third eye types. I have no problem with juniper berries after they flavor gin, but they lack appeal in their native dress.

After extensive research I found the local feed store to be the most appealing.

Parking is no problem. The odor of cracked corn, dog food and bird seed assures the concerned customer that all is not yet plastic. Here in this world of chambray blue shirts, one size-fits-all caps and cheerful clerks who never question your report of the poundage you have removed from the scale, I feel at home.

One customer observing me pay for a order of feed, asks the question: "Where's your outfit?"

Trying to dodge the question, I reply, "Just on the edge of town."

Then again he asks. "How many head you run?"

"I figure about six hundred," I guess.

"Herefords?"

"No. Blue jays."

You never heard me say a word when the Arizona Legislature neglected to create a paid state holiday honoring Martin Luther King, Jr. I was quiet as a carpet mouse when they dipped into the lottery funds to bail out several poorly managed counties. When a now-infamous Phoenix developer was asked by the legislature to stop using our drinking water for his phony lagoons and told the Legislature to go to hell, I never let out a peep. When annually the beverage dealers prevent a much-needed bottle bill from being enacted by hosting a few key legislators to a tuna salad sandwich and a glass of iced tea, I bit my lips.

But this time they've gone too far. The character of this legislation is so outrageous, it has been hushed up. The bill designates an official Arizona mammal, reptile, amphibian and fish. Most states have done likewise, even going a bit further and naming an official insect (I know a politician who would be ideal in the role.) The idea is fine and gives a keener identity to Arizona, but the mammal, reptile, amphibian and fish that the legislators selected make me wonder what planet they live on.

If you were going to pick an official mammal for the State of Arizona, what would you pick? A javelina? Desert bighorn? Kaibab squirrel? What do you think those dingbats picked? Are you ready for this? A ringtail cat! *(Bassariscus astutus)*. Can you believe it? That's what Tom Mix used to call the bad guys before the movies let the language get a little spicier. The ringtail cat is a first cousin to the coatimundi and the raccoon. They are all a bunch of thieves, tipping over garbage cans and eating gold fish out of lily ponds.

Now let me tell you what they picked for the official reptile. The ridgenose rattlesnake! *(Crotalus willardi)*. Most of the people from Wall Street to Waxahachie, Texas think Arizona has no plant, insect or animal that doesn't sting, stick, stalk, slink or stink.

That's all we need, a ridgenose rattler coiled on the marble floor under the Capitol rotunda. The official reptile should be the colorful native lizard, the Gila Monster, once the logo of the Arizona National Guard. Like all natives, he has beady eyes, bad breath and doesn't want any more people around to disturb him. The official fish is the Arizona trout. *(Salmo apache)*. My choice would have been the verde mudsucker, but I will admit the trout tastes much better.

I have no idea where these dunderheads were when they selected Arizona's official amphibian. It must have been a midnight session in the cellar of a saloon. They named the Arizona tree frog. I have lived here all my life and the only Arizona tree frog I ever saw was on the parking lot of a big city restaurant, late one rainy night. At least that's what my friend said it was, and she excelled in high school biology.

As far as I know, Arizona doesn't have an official fossil, and that's just as well. I am afraid some wise guy just might nominate me.

Gee, I don't know Stanley, you mean what one thing has made the biggest improvement in our lives in the last fifty years?"

"Yeah, that's what I mean, like I think that maybe those big RVs you see on the road have done more than canned beer to make people happy.

"Stanley, I can't agree with you. I think Winnebagos have wrecked more marriages than twin beds and cigar smoke combined."

"Well how about Scotch tape?" asked Stanley.

"I admit that Scotch tape has made life easier but certainly the polio vaccine was a much greater contribution."

"Well, what do *you* think has been the greatest improvement?"

I was quick to respond. "No question about it as far as Arizona is concerned — refrigeration. Air conditioning has changed the whole pattern of life in Arizona."

"Well, it made a big difference," said Stanley, "but you can't call that an improvement. If air conditioning had never been invented, Phoenix wouldn't have a traffic problem and you could get a motel room for five bucks a night."

"Improvement, like beauty, is in the eye of the beholder," I philosophized.

"Well what do you think about king cab pickups, frozen dinners and zippers on Levi's?"

"You are doing better Stanley, you got two out of three, but I would rather have a can of Spam than a frozen dinner."

"Well, you got to admit," said Stanley, "that freeways and paint rollers and fast food restaurants have saved people a lot of time."

"I have nothing against saving time Stanley, but I think that the modern, standardized, corporate hamburger is an atrocity rivaling the Holocaust."

"Well, name a couple of improvements," said Stanley.

"For openers how about health insurance and smoke alarms?"

"Yeah, they're both good. How about suburban development programs?"

"I can't really see that as progress, Stanley. For the

last fifty years we have had millions of Americans move from the urban slums to the suburban sprawl. Now we are trying to get some of those people to move back into the city centers and breathe life into them."

"Well, if we are going to enter this contest we both have to come up with one thing that we think has done more than anything else to make life better. What are you going to put down?"

"Running shoes," I answered.

"Running shoes?" said Stanley. "You don't run. Why are you going to pick running shoes?"

"Because, Stanley, they are comfortable. Since humans have been on Earth, uncomfortable footwear has caused more misery than ragweed and the Internal Revenue Service. Running shoes get my vote. What's yours?"

Stanley stared into space for several seconds. Then as if he had received a divine revelation, he said, "Disposable diapers. No more soaking, rinsing, washing and folding. Parents nowadays have a cinch."

"Stanley, I bet you are going to win the contest. What is the first prize?"

"A years supply of disposable diapers. Say, do you know anybody who's fixin' to have a baby?"

Within the past several years the group-sponsored horseback ride has enjoyed an ever-increasing popularity. Most of these organized rides cover a formidable distance through an area of great beauty or historical significance. The Santa Barbara, California outing and the Wickenburg, Scottsdale, and White Mountain rides in Arizona, are just a few examples of this type of annual event, and usually there is an eager list of riders awaiting an invitation to join in.

Most of these rides are sponsored by some organization whose sole purpose is one big annual event. It is done with flair and novelty which compel the riders to return year after year.

A group of men in the Nogales area recently founded such a ride. They had all the necessary prerequisites; good horsemen, camp cooks, a plethora of cut-rate liquor stores and trails which traverse an intriguing international border.

Tom Hunt of the Rail X Ranch near Patagonia is a member of this group. He has all the skills including the ability to shoe a horse. Recently in preparation for the ride he was shoeing a favorite horse. He was seventy-five percent finished with the job. Only one rear hoof remained to be done, and this hoof had been clipped and filed flat and smooth with a coarse rasp in preparation for the setting of the final shoe.

When Tom released this last hoof of the old horse to pick up the shoe and nails, the horse set his newly polished hoof firmly on the toe of Tom's boot. While some pain was experienced, no great damage was done. Tom only leaned into the horse to urge him off the pressure point. The horse responded by leaning back into him as he had been trained. By now the pain was beginning to mount. Rather than call for help from Cotton Benton who was sitting on a nail keg a few feet away, Tom, in agony, took the huge metal rasp in his hand and applied it to a convenient portion of the horse where rasps are rarely used.

When the horse shot off Tom's foot he did so with such force that he took the big toenail off Tom's foot as cleanly as if it had been pulled by a sadistic dentist. By now, what little composure Tom had been able to keep intact was gone. With his best Olympian effort he threw the heavy rasp in the direction of the disappearing horse. Cotton Benton had witnessed very little of this quick sequence of events. He was still seated on the nail keg in deep concentration rolling a cigarette. He had just dammed a little saliva on the tip of his tongue and was preparing to slide the edge of the cigarette paper through it when the rasp hit him full force between the eyes.

The Nogales ride will begin a little later this year. Tom Hunt can still only wear one boot. He has a horse who needs one more shoe. And Cotton Benton, who was one of the best damn camp cooks on the Mexican border, is convinced he was kicked in the head by a horse.

© 1994 Bill Ahrendt

CHAPTER

A Little Ruff around the Edges

The experts can give you almost any statistic you want. Now, five hundred years after Columbus set foot on a New World beach, this question has come up. Just how many Indians were living in the North American continent when the Genoa navigator dropped anchor?

Anthropologist are no different from psychiatrists, lawyers and Democrats when it comes to eclectic opinions. I prefer the anthropologists who put the pre-Columbian population high, somewhere between ten to twelve million. If you are inclined to think this figure is a bit exaggerated, keep this in mind. Today, from the Atlantic to the Pacific, pottery shards are still plentiful on undisturbed ground.

Also, the area in question includes Mexico, which had an extensive indigenous population at the time of Columbus. The culture was well-advanced even by European standards. These natives were tribal in social structure and lived in well-defined territories. Most farmed, growing maize, beans, squash and corn.

They had no draft animals, but hitched dogs to a travois. They had little need to travel far afield for game. Extensive travel was regarded as an act of war. The horse was unknown. The wheel, uninvented.

In the field of literature, toward the end of the nineteenth of the century, the pioneer Anglo was the good guy; the Indian, a sinister savage not to be trusted.

This genre of cowboy-and-Indian literature was nourished by the pulp magazines for nearly half a century. However, there were exceptions. Elliot Arnold's *Blood Brother* pictured Cochise as a decent human being. Theretofore, Cochise had lived in literature as inhuman, deceitful and cruel.

Oliver La Farge's *Laughing Boy* took the reader into the mind and spirit of a young Navajo. Our ethnocentrism toward Navajo diet, personal hygiene and values softened.

The mutation continued in the 1960s and '70s. The turn-of-the-century plot was reversed. The Anglo pioneer was pictured as an insensitive, rapacious, land-grabbing clod. In this time of cultural upheaval the role reversal sold books.

The western writers who were inclined to be pro-Anglo have suffered a long drought. Now once again the tide has turned. This time, both Anglo and Indian appear in a realistic light. This is more informative and honest.

An Anglo friend of mine who is, in my opinion, a revisionist and pro-Indian to a fault, blames all the tragedies which occurred during the westward expansion on the Anglo. When I disagreed with him in a rather firm manner, he defended his thesis well.

He told me that when the Indians were running the country, there was no national debt, no inflation, no taxes and no AIDS. The air was clean, the waters unpolluted and the women did all the work.

I may reassess my thinking.

It is one of the few places on either the South or the North rims of the Grand Canyon where you can stand and look straight down. No benches, no shelves, no juts, straight down. Three thousand feet. Toroweap Point is a Paiute word which must be an expletive in their language.

I've always liked what the ten-year-old tourist boy wrote in the signature book at Toroweap: "Today, I spit a mile!"

Toroweap is located on the North Rim near Vulcan's Thorne and directly above the dangerous and dramatic Lava Falls. From the paved Arizona Route 389 west of Fredonia, sixty-eight miles of dirt road cross Antelope Valley and the Kanab Plateau past the east slope of Mt. Trumbull to the rim.

We camped on bedrock, surrounded by 360 degrees of pastel plateaus, cedar-studded mesas and distant monoliths. Waxy prickly pear blooms and rose, yellow, red and fuchsia wildflowers gave both color and warmth to our camp. One of our fearsome threesome, a perfectionist in every sense of the word, added to the glory of each morning by brewing the finest coffee I have ever tasted.

He buys the beans from an importer in Seattle and grinds them himself fresh as needed. With a small French stove and filtered pot, he delighted my day but destroyed my future. From now on every cup of coffee I have is going to taste like it came from a Texas truck stop.

It is safe to say that Toroweap doesn't have the number of tourists that are normally found between El Tovar and the Hopi House. Therefore, we were quite surprised when a chap walked into our camp one afternoon. He was a large man, well dressed for the field, with handsome, crew cut gray hair.

His German-accented English, while not perfect, was considerably better than the average American college freshman. His bearing was so commanding I suspect he took early retirement when World War II ended. The man had a problem. He and his wife were touring from their home in Bremen. They had flown to Los Angeles, rented a car, set out for the Grand Canyon.

From study of a road map he had determined the shortest route to the rim. Ah, the wonder of a German mind. After he and his frau had viewed the Canyon he discovered his rental car had a dead battery. Hence, he came to our camp for help.

I had neither a jumper cable nor a Ph.D., but both my friends did. Between the psychologist, the archeologist and the Teuton they managed to start the car. The next morning the German couple broke camp, convinced the Grand Canyon was deeper than the Bismarck. You had to hand it to the German couple. They bypassed Disneyland and headed straight to Las Vegas.

After that and the Grand Canyon, what else is there in America?

First is a dangerous word. Any writer should be cautious in its use and, if possible, avoid it entirely. The popular expression, "first ever" is another bastard child of television. It adds redundancy to a risky superlative. First is all that is necessary, but it is dangerous.

Several years ago a young lady wrote an article about a balloon ascension. Hot air ballooning had become a popular sport and the young lady, a *Prescott Courier* reporter, wrote a fine story about a modern, local balloon ascension. She made the mistake of saying it was the first. To her eternal credit she did not say the first ever.

The first? Several oldtimers frowned. Some grumped and groused. One, in a kind and articulate manner, told the story.

Gail I. Gardner as a child had witnessed a lady aerialist, dressed in shocking tinsel-spangled tights, climb into a wicker basket and rise from the surface of the Prescott Plaza in her hot air balloon. Gail described the scene. The tights seemed to hold more fascination for him than the balloon.

"I was just a young boy," he said, "and it was the first time I found out what a woman looked like when they didn't have one of those long black dresses on."

In preparing for her flight the lady used the kind of language seldom heard in Sunday school. Well, some of the words. But with different inflection. This, too, gave young Gail an insight to the realities of life.

The lady aerialist and her balloon landed at Fort Whipple a few miles from downtown. Gail thought it was about 1899 or perhaps 1900; it was on the Fourth of July.

I didn't say it was the first hot air balloon flight in Prescott. He did.

Now a word about the "first" heavier-than-air flying machine in these parts. In Ruth Reinhold's book *Sky Pioneering: Arizona in Aviation History,* the author states that the tiny craft was shipped to Prescott via rail for the Yavapai County Fair in 1915.

One afternoon, it was rolled out in front of the grandstand, and as a volunteer ground crew held the craft's wings, the pilot revved the engine up to full speed. When released at the pilot's signal, the airplane took to the air at a rather sharp angle climbing to a height of fifty feet. Pilot and plane circled the half-mile track several times, then landed at the starting point.

It was the first ever flight from Prescott.

No, it was the first airplane flight from Prescott.

Well, maybe it wasn't the first.

Who knows?

The practice of law has created more genuine characters than Walt Disney could have, had he lived another century. Contemporary society seems to have discouraged, or at least diluted, some of the colorful, flamboyant practitioners of the past. A century ago, many lawyers, especially those who operated in the American West, were both scholars and dramatists. In today's sterile society, the legal scholar is respected, the dramatist, suspected. It is a cultural loss.

The first officials of the new State of Arizona were elected in the fall of 1911. Among them was a handsome young man, Henry Fountain Ashurst, who would come to be known in the United States Senate as "The Silver-Tongued Orator." Born in Nevada, Henry came to Arizona as an infant and grew to manhood in a log cabin [honestly] south of Flagstaff. Like Lincoln, he read his beloved books by fireplace light. His ability to recall and quote a wide range of literature from Plato to Twain, was impressive. Henry was admitted to the bar without suffering the indignities of a law school. Before he went to the Senate, he did indeed practice law in both Flagstaff and Prescott. Ashurst's speeches or portions of them have become collector items. The most extensive body of Ashurstiana was compiled by Representative Morris Udall.

In 1908 young Ashurst was defending a man accused of stealing a calf. The case was to be tried before Justice of the Peace, Henry Waltron, in Winslow, Arizona Territory. Judge Waltron had a meat market in Winslow and the courtroom was in a room in the rear of the market. Here, Henry Fountain Ashurst made his now famous opening statement.

"Your honor, as I approached the trial of this case today, my heart was burdened with crushing and gloomy forebodings. The immense responsibility of my client's welfare bowed me down with apprehensions. A cold fear gripped my heart as I dwelt upon the possibility that through some oversight or shortcoming of mine there might ensue dreadful consequences to my client, and I shrank within myself as the ordeal became more imminent. Yet the nearer my uncertain steps brought me to this tribunal of justice, distinguished as it has been for years as the one court of the rugged West where fame attended the wisdom and justice of the decisions of your honor, a serene confidence came to my troubled emotions, and the raging waters of tumultuous floods that had surged hotly by a moment before were stilled.

"Your honor, I was no longer appalled. I no longer

feared the issue in this case. Aye, I reflected that throughout the long years of your administration as judge, there had grown up here a halo as it were of honor and glory illuminating your honor's record, eloquent of a fame as deserved as that of the chastity of Caesar's wife, a fame that will augment with the flight of years and with increasing luster light the pathway of humanity down the ages so long as the heaving billows of the stormy Mediterranean shall beat vainly upon the beetling cliffs of Gibraltar."

Judge Waltron: "Sit down, Mr. Ashurst. You can't blow any smoke up this court's ass."

Some cynics who claim to be friends of mine are not going to believe this. Those infidels who think of me as a burnt bacon and broken yoke chef will be envious when they see how my culinary artistry has advanced.

I spent a few days in Mexico recently at the home of a friend in the colonial village of Alamos. My friend is a bachelor, but that is not his single blessing. He lives in a lovely restored hacienda, has an extensive vegetable garden and possesses the skills of a fine chef. While I was grateful for the delicious creations my host placed on the table every evening, I ate very sparingly as my principal concern was the preparation of the food rather than the consumption.

While others in our little group frittered away their time plunked on the patio in the shade of the portal, I seized the opportunity for self-improvement. Abandoning the cooling breeze, clinking ice and idle chatter of pre-dinner festivities, I remained at the elbow of our chef-host for a transfusion of his knowledge despite the heat and concentration of a creative kitchen.

I was delighted, one evening, when Walter announced he was going to prepare paella, the traditional Spanish dish, limited only by the imagination of the cook. Rice and saffron are mandatory but other than these, all sorts of meats, fish and vegetables may be used to bring into full bloom an entree fit for a conquistador. Back home, I had just purchased a paella pan, so I monitored every culinary move. I jotted no notes, as I had once taken a memory course, but I can't recall just when or where.

Some paella cooks would lead you to believe the process is time-consuming and difficult. Not so. Walter and I prepared it quickly and with little effort. Somewhat as Van Cliburn would snap out a sonata.

First you put the paella pan on the stove. You light the burner. In the pan is a little olive oil. In this you brown the chicken thighs or wings or maybe it was necks. Set these aside when browned. Now, put a couple of handfuls of cooked rice in the pan and kind of stir-fry it. Gently add a few mustard greens or fresh spinach, whatever.

Now put the chicken back in the pan and add shrimp, scallops and hearts of artichokes. Don't panic, keep stirring. If you detect a little drying, add a little wine. In a separate saucepan simmer the saffron. (You may have to take out a second mortgage to buy the saffron.)

Now add some bits of sausage — Polish, Italian, Pennsylvania will do. Taste as you go so you will know when it's done. Strain the saucepan of saffron and add to the above. Serve in the pan and garnish with pimiento and olives. It makes the finest paella you ever put in your mouth. I start tomorrow.

The economic base of Arizona used to be described succinctly and accurately as the Four Cs—Cotton, Copper, Cattle and Climate. Three of the four now run at the rear of the field and the fourth, climate, has taken a new identification, now known as tourism.

The economics of cotton farming must be self-destructive, for what once was a major portion of Arizona agriculture is now all but invisible. The high cost of water, abundant cheap synthetics and labor problems have driven King Cotton from his throne.

The revolution in electronics, the micro-chip, foreign imports and, finally, environmental concerns, have caused the copper companies to concentrate on economic survival rather than political influence. Phelps Dodge retreated from the canyons of Manhattan to circle their headquarters wagons on Central Avenue in Phoenix.

The climate business has adapted and flourished. The days of the dude ranch are all but gone, but filling the gap is an ever-increasing supply of sophisticated resort facilities complete with French chefs. Lifestyles and leisure time have created a huge demand for tourist attractions and accommodations. Arizona has much to offer and the tourist dollar will continue to be a principal portion of our economic base.

That leaves the last C, cattle. A romantic industry is now tormented by more bad guys than Tom Mix dealt with in a lifetime. Raising cattle requires as much business acumen as a seat of the stock exchange but offers little opportunity for arbitrage. In the Sun Belt (or Gun Belt as my effete friends refer to it), it takes fifty to sixty acres to support one cow. That land has to be either purchased, leased or in hand with taxes due. That makes it kind of tough to compete with real estate developers and condominium builders. Then too, in today's world, the rancher is frequently assailed by recent liberal arts graduates who have by some miracle become range management experts. They accuse him of land abuse, riparian rape and tumbleweed molestation. The truth is that the experienced representative cattleman is a fine steward of the land. He has to be. His livelihood depends upon it.

The cattle business today is suffering from declining beef sales. I recently talked with the family manager of a large ranch in Northern Arizona. He said that beef demand dwindled year by year because of changing dietary habits such as avoidance of fatty meat. Once, marbled beef was considered the finest; now it is shunned. If the trend continues, he thinks he may abandon the cattle business for other fields. The great hope for the cattle business, he claims, is the genetic progress to develop a much leaner breed of good beef cattle.

I don't think dietary fads or even the cost of beef compared with foods is mainly to blame for the decline of beef sales. There's been a radical change in the way beef is sold. The butcher back of the counter is a sight now seldom seen. To watch him prepare a roast, steak, or even two pounds of ground chili beef and hand it to you wrapped in clean butcher paper, was a social ceremony. Styrofoam trays containing unknown chunks of beef covered with plastic wrap and computer priced, just don't jangle my juices. I believe a few good butchers could save more ranches than a few good bankers.

Let me pose a question. Looking back on your life, what three people you have met or admired, have made the most favorable impression on you?

This question popped into my mind the other day and the hardest problem was to limit to three. In doing so, I had to eliminate some fine individuals. People like John Wayne, who in spite of his film success, was a modest, outgoing man who always took the trouble to ask about you and direct the conversation toward your area of interest.

I liked the image Wayne projected in his films. You could count on him. He worried the hell out of me at times, but he always got there just in the nick of time and in spite of horrendous odds, gave the bad guys what they so well deserved.

He treated his horse like a horse and a woman like a lady. He was an intensely patriotic man and proud of it. In public he was an upstanding model, honest and as refreshing and natural as rain. In private he was a warm, family-loving man who knew how lucky he was to go as far as he did "on a half a tank of talent."

Now, the three I decided on. All are deceased. In my lifetime I met two of them; the other, I knew as a close friend and teacher.

America never had a finer hero than Charles Lindbergh. When he landed at Le Bourget Airfield outside Paris on May 21, 1927, the stoic Swede became a world figure. He was awarded the Congressional Medal of Honor, wrote a best seller, *We,* and toured the country under the auspices of the Guggenheim Foundation.

When his infant son was murdered he became a sad recluse. Before World War II, Lindbergh tried to tell his government about the nature of communism and the effectiveness of the Luftwaffe but was ignored and insulted. Once we were in the war, his numerous contributions to military intelligence were invaluable. History proved his point.

He hated the hero's role. The last few years of his life he had little if any social contact. His interest turned to the mysteries of nature.

Gladys Reichard was the most amazing woman I have ever met. She was an anthropologist who taught at Barnard, a woman's college within the complex of Columbia University. In the early 1930s she came west every summer to do research on the Navajo Reservation, and it was here I was fortunate when she took me under her wing.

She was a pure scientist, devoted to her work well beyond what I regarded as the realm of reason. She taught me the valuable lesson to judge "other people" by their values and standards rather than mine.

I was fifteen years old and had never heard of ethnocentrism and certainly didn't know that I was infected with it. If Gladys Reichard didn't eliminate it from my system, she certainly diluted it.

I began to regard Indians as people. Even Navajos. Today forty-five years after her death, she is regarded as one of the foremost American anthropologists.

And finally, he used to come to the Prescott Frontier Days Rodeo years ago when he was a national personality. He would sit on the fence and stand behind the chutes with the cowboys...his kind of people.

He was the highest paid entertainer in the country at the time. He also ran a daily "squib column" in most of America's newspapers. Much of what he said and wrote those many years ago is still relevant today.

When he died at Point Barrow, Alaska, in 1935, America lost a beloved leader. My father and I were having lunch at the Harvey House in Ash Fork when the waitress, weeping, brought the news. We also wept.

His shrewd satire and homey philosophy took a touch of immortality: "Now I know what a statesman is. He's a dead politician. What we need is more statesmen."

In light of the biographies of some of our deceased presidents, Will Rogers' remark of decades ago still rings true.

"More men have been elected between sundown and sunup, than ever were elected between sunup and sundown."

Will could see into the future: "Politics is becoming so expensive that it takes a lot of money even to get beat."

Among many others, these three I loved and respected.

Moenkopi was the setting — a puebloan enclave surrounded by the Navajo Nation in far Northern Arizona. If it had occurred a day or two later the scene would have been quite different. The timing was perfect, schools were still in session, the holiday weekend had not reached its full thrust, and the Kleenex bushes were not yet in bloom. It was an Indian ceremony for Indians. Only seven *bahanas* (non-Hopis) were there. They were the invited guests known to be fully aware of Amerind custom and amenities. The white women guests wore dresses and the knowledgeable men guests never touched the food until it was time to eat.

It was a kind of corn dance to express thanks for the winter of rain and to offer a prayer in hopes that summer, too, might nurture the crops of the Hopi. Forty-two Kachinas ran across the bluff to the plaza. Below their masks some had the small smooth bodies of ten-year-olds and others showed signs of seventy winters and starch diets. Where the masks met the shoulders of the dancers, the union was hidden by a ring of fresh green fir boughs; more of these symbols of rich growth were tucked into the tops of their cotton loin cloths and tied by bright wool yarn around the calves of their legs. Every dancer had a fine silver *gato* (bracelet) around his left wrist, and one participant whose waist had exceeded the length of his concha belt, joined the ancient ends with a bright new stainless steel cowboy buckle with the brass design of a bucking bronco. From some of the wooden ears of the Kachina masks hung turquoise earrings or woven wool pendants, but two or three less substantive members of the dance team had cone-shaped Dixie cups dangling upside down as a twentieth century substitute.

Four times during the day the forty-two Kachinas came to the plaza and danced and droned their low, humming chants to implore the gods. Three corn maidens knelt in the four directions and in perfect rhythm scraped a dry sheep scapula along a notched hardwood stick to add noisy emphasis to the appeal.

Each time the Kachinas came to the plaza, they brought with them the practical gifts of a not-rich reservation economy. Halfway through each stylized ceremony they stopped and passed these gifts out to the spectators who had ringed the arena with their pickup trucks and folding camp chairs. No gratitude was expressed when the gift was received. For the Hopi, gratitude would have destroyed the spirit of giving.

Canned fruit, homemade bread, watermelon and sacks of Navajo flour were offered and accepted.

In the late afternoon, the Kachinas went back to the Kiva. The aluminum camp chairs were folded. These and the gifts were placed in the rear of the pickups, the tailgates were slammed shut and the people went home. A huge red cloud of dust ascended over the plaza and hung there as a final supplication. Summer had come to the Hopi land.

Last week I received a well-written letter from Kip Dickie (Ms.? Mrs.? Mr.?). Dickie has resided in Prescott several months and hinted, but never admitted, he/she had entered Arizona by crossing the Colorado River. This indicated to me that Dickie's former home had been LaLa Land. Beyond this burden of personal history, Dickie may be a native of the scorched and shaky earth, riot capital, hope of the dismal Dodgers and Charles Manson look-alikes state.

In any event, Dickie is not yet acculturated to the local protocols and practices. While some disenchantment with local attitudes toward transplants was expressed, the principal complaint of Dickie was how to pronounce the name — Prescott, the old territorial capital of Arizona.

Why Dickie directed his/her inquiry to me, I know not. The various "correct" pronunciations that had been offered by editors, historians, linguists, curators, archivists, the mayor, and eight bartenders, all conflict and confuse the issue. As yet, the mayor can't even spell it.

Now, the answer is not a simple one. The truth is, there are several pronunciations of Prescott, depending on various factors. Backtrackers to Prescott, by that, I mean those new arrivals from the Pacific coast, seem to prefer the pronunciation, Presskit. This anomaly may be a result of the California school system or a chronic throat condition due to constant exposure to smog.

The affluent, old money, Ivy League types, have a slow almost erotic pronunciation, but duplicated as Press-Scott. While I do not find this offensive, it seems somehow pretentious.

Those hardy souls who have pulled their U-Hauls in from their former homes in the Bible Belt of our great nation have all settled on the pronunciation — Pre-scit. It is a short and pinched version of the name. I suspect it is rooted in an unedited, mimeographed church bulletin which they have been exposed to since childhood.

Now we should touch on the native pronunciation. First however, in Prescott, anyone who has been here long enough to pay off his new pickup, is considered a native.

Having had that defined, a native unless *borracho* normally says Presscuit, as in biscuit. This however, has been challenged over the years by academic types. The result of this controversy has been an anti-intellectual environment nourished by local radio.

Often the problem of the present can be answered by the past. Certainly this is true in this case. When the name of this new city was being considered, several were suggested. Perhaps we had better ask the city administration to reconsider what has proven to be a bad decision. The town was almost named Granite City. Certainly an honest and descriptive name, easy to pronounce. A native of Venice suggested Venezia and when this was rejected he affixed the name to his mining claim in the Bradshaw Mountains.

When the meeting to name the town was held May 30, 1864, Richard McCormick, secretary of the territory, offered the name Prescott after William Hickling Prescott, the historian. McCormick was always a troublemaker. Goodwin City was an offering to honor the governor, when in fact he had done nothing but show up. An elderly miner suggested Gimletville. Why? *¿Quien sabe?* There is a gimlet cocktail and a gimlet tool.

Within days now, petitions will be in the banks and bars, demanding that the mayor and city council change the name from Prescott to Gimletville, as it should have been in the first place. If you can't pronounce Gimletville maybe you had better move back to Cucamonga.

This story has a happy ending. Beyond that, it also serves as a morality play, demonstrating the power and security of a cohesive family unit, an immortal faith and unsurrendered personal integrity.

Sometime in the middle of this century, two little brown brothers started selling chiles by the roadside in Española, New Mexico. The summer sun soon required a big umbrella to shade both the chiles and children. Out of this initial foray into the world of free enterprise, emerged what became a regional treasure, El Paragua Restaurant.

From 1963 until 1990, for twenty-seven years the Atencio family owned and operated El Paragua (The Parasol) serving the finest of traditional New Mexican cuisine with the warmth and care of a kindergarten teacher. The message of excellence traveled with a speed that only the human tongue can provide. Customers came. Supreme Court justices, film stars, socialites, artists and less famed, pushed the carved door open time and time again.

Success can be a seducer. In 1990, the Atencio family opened a second restaurant, Las Brazas, in Cuyamungue, a few miles down the road toward Santa Fe. The combination of separation of facilities, a nose dive economy and a shortage of the Atencio touch, introduced the dragon of bankruptcy. The family patron, Luis Atencio, was forced to close the doors and face the music.

For the next two years, each crisis descending on the Atencio family was conquered by character. The nine children and their children worked. Three of the daughters and their children set up a small stand on the parking lot of the boarded up El Paragua with the proceeds going in the family pot. Every member of the family cooperated with the court-appointed trustee.

Once a month, the family recited the Rosary at Capilla de Santo Niño Chapel, not far from the site where the world's best menudo was once served. Their prayers brought progress. The $520,000 debt was reduced. Tax liens, interest, the State of New Mexico and a stern banker were paid, promised or both. The road back was long, rutted and dusty, but there was a road.

In the Roman Catholic faith, Saint Jude is the patron saint of lost causes. Saint Jude and a bank beyond the borders of New Mexico finally enabled the Atencios to buy back El Paragua and begin again.

This is not the first essay I have done on El Paragua. I did one years ago and the Atencios enlarged and displayed it on the wall. I have been a guest there many times. When a friend and I pulled onto an unkempt parking lot and looked at the sad sight of boarded-up windows, it was like standing at the grave of a dear friend.

Courage, character and a faith from here to infinity have reopened El Paragua. May their God be as good to the Atencios as the Atencios have been to their creditors and customers. *Vaya con Díos*.

My wish is that you will read this on Christmas Day, surrounded by those you love and those who love you. May your home be warm, and you be well dressed and nourished. At your fingertips you will have the finest music, drama, entertainers and sports events in the world. Transportation and communication will be globally available on demand. There will be an absence of danger; and at least, a period of peace.

Now let us go back to a Christmas about 150 miles northeast of Prescott and some twenty miles east of the present-day Flagstaff before Arizona was even an American territory. It is Christmas, 1853 and a young army lieutenant, Amiel Weeks Whipple, is exploring a possible route for a railroad west from Fort Smith to Los Angeles. An Arizona fort will later bear his name and he will serve as a Brigadier General in the Civil War. He will be dreadfully wounded in battle at Chancellorsville, Virginia and die of his wounds on May 7, 1868, three years after the war's end.

On December 23, 1853, Lt. Whipple and his party have marched through a snowstorm all day. Finally, they come to Cosnino Caves, a sheltered spot on the forest edge; water, grass and wood are abundant. When they began the day's march, the temperature was three below zero; now late in the day, the sun has melted the snow from the southern slopes.

Here the men make camp and elect to remain three days to celebrate Christmas. On the twenty-fourth, hunters go out for turkey, deer or bear, but most return empty-handed. The party has adequate food, however, and the cooks prepare a sumptuous dinner for Christmas Eve. Some foresighted individuals before leaving Albuquerque, have secured a carefully packed crate of eggs in a wagon. Others have brought wine and rum and several kinds of delicacies to enhance the season. A huge camp kettle is hung over the fire and within it, eggs, rum, wine, water and odd, but inspirational additives, joined together bubbling and steaming.

Mollhausen, a German artist who accompanied the expedition, later describes the scene, telling how the men dipped their cups into this hot and potent Christmas cheer.

"The men sat around the fires and smoked and drank and sang. Toasts and jokes followed one another rapidly, hearts became lighter, the blood ran more swiftly in the veins, and all present joined in such a lively chorus as echoed far and wide through the ravines, and must have sadly interfered with the night's rest of the sleeping turkeys."

Whipple's report tells how the old mountain man and guide for the expedition, Antoine Leroux, and his servant, a Crow Indian, perform duets, fandango style. Fireworks, which had been hidden in a wagon, light the frozen December sky. Several tall, ponderosa pines are set on fire, sending flames and sparks high into the air. Some of the Mexican packers who had once been prisoners of the Navajos perform their version of a Navajo dance. Finally, the many voices become subdued. Toasts and poems, once recited, are never long remembered. The songs sink into silence and the last flames flicker and die.

Christmas morning, 1853, Cosnino Caves welcomes dawn with the field thermometer registering zero. The camp remains quiet and intact. Mollhausen describes the mood:

"Christmas day was spent in perfect quiet, in thinking over times and our distant homes."

So there won't be any misunderstanding, let me first admit, I am an Anglophile. I am aware that the history of England is that of profit from both defeat and victory. I have always admired the typical British understatement and studied reaction. Their politics display more passion than their love lives, and their values are commendable. A dignified, soft-spoken religion, fine horses, reliable engines, warm clothing and spectacular gardens. But above all, the English have the gift of turning garbage into gold.

Take the English custom of Boxing Day, for example. Some smart Englishman invented Boxing Day to solve the problem of unwanted Christmas gifts. If we Americans get a purple bow tie for Christmas we just suffer. Not the English. The first weekday following Christmas is a holiday.

Boxing Day, they call it, and it is observed by giving boxes and gifts to household help and service personnel. You can give the tie to the gardener. But if you are really fond of the guy who has been taking care of the garden, you can give him something else and return the bow tie to the store for credit. Only the English could solve the problem with such a civilized solution and take a day off to do it.

The English always have an answer. Real estate has

been moving a little slow over there lately, so Strutt and Parker, one of England's leading real estate firms together with the Manorial Society decided to auction off fifty "Lords of the Manor" titles. Not the manor, just the title.

There seems to be a world demand for titles these days — an Arab with nothing but money, a Japanese manufacturer who wants name and recognition, or a retired Wall Street lawyer now living in Miami Beach. The auction was held, and several titles were sold in the range of 7,000 to 10,000 pounds, about $10,000 to $14,000. The English peddle these kinds of intangibles to eager buyers like Lord and Lady Bill Joe Buckner of Standing Stud Ranch, Fort Worth, Texas.

Ironically, the Brits had the manorial titles forced on them in 1066 when Duke William of Normandy conquered England. The Battle of Hastings broke the back of the British and William of Normandy brought such advances to the British Isles as the French language and feudalism.

Though the Brits never did learn to speak French, they did like the feudal system and the result was lord and vassal. From this developed the manorial system and the Lords of the Manor. You have to admire a people who are invaded and subjected to the edict of the conqueror from which they gain land and titles. Then, 900 years later, they sell the title to some well-heeled egocentric for $10,000.

Such enterprise gives new meaning to that old war time chant: "There will always be an England."

Reading newspapers daily and turning on the evening news with a compulsiveness bordering on addiction tends to generate cynicism. Not much of what we see and hear is inspiring or comforting.

Every day, somewhere in the world, people are killing or being killed. Murder and rape are commonplace in our villages as well as our cities. Dishonesty in positions of public trust is epidemic. Wall Street has no more morality, character or integrity than Skid Row. Rudeness is the norm and common courtesy endangered. No wonder we feel vulnerable, defensive, antisocial. But then, at unexpected times and places, we sometimes see a sign of civilization. A kindness, a courtesy, makes an unexpected public appearance. A dim flame, a hope of humanity flickers, if not to restore, at least to retain the little faith we have left.

The intersection of east Camelback and Twenty-fourth Street in Phoenix is not known as the womb of human kindness. At every phase and change of the traffic lights, hundreds of harried drivers compete for time and traffic flow. Silent curses, obscene gestures and clenched fists often are in evidence. Crunched car combat is not unknown.

This turmoil derives from personal stress. Many of those who pass here have problems, bad problems. Problems that involve family, money, job security or health. Motorists are naturally egocentric. They are in a hurry, unconcerned with others' problems. It is the normal behavior pattern of a pressured society.

I had just left the parking lot and was headed west on Camelback. I was in the right-hand lane so I could turn on Twenty-fourth Street and head for home. A small, concrete island separates this lane from the mass of westbound traffic. I had a green light, but I saw a young man standing on the corner holding a long white cane. He semed bewildered, in trying to cross the street.

I turned on my emergency blinkers and stopped. Then I saw his companion on the concrete island crying, holding on to her guide dog. For what seemed an eternity, every car about to leave or enter that intersection stopped. No horns were honked. No oaths were uttered. No fists were clenched. Time and traffic became unimportant. Personal problems suddenly appeared petty. Concerns focused on someone else. Presently, an alert young police officer calmly walked through the maze of immobile automobiles, told the young man to stand still, and helped the young lady up. Then with the young couple and the dog in hand, he escorted them across the street. Slowly, cautiously, the traffic began to move again.

People smiled at one another. They nodded. Some wept.

Thomas Harriot, an English scientist, published the first American book in English in 1588. Titled, *A Briefe and True Report of the New Found Land of Virginia,* it described the natural resources perceived in the new region.

Today, four centuries after this first book was published and circulated, we still have present in our society the tragic condition of illiteracy. The ability to read is a golden gate to the mysteries of the world and its peoples.

No one knew this better than the frail-bodied Sequoyah, a half-breed Cherokee Indian. In 1809, when he was thirty-nine years old, Sequoyah began working on a Cherokee syllabary after observing the whites transfer information and various messages by means of symbols placed on paper. For twelve years he labored without family support or tribal encouragement. In 1821, Sequoyah appeared before the Cherokee Council to win adoption of his syllabary.

Thereafter thousands of his people learned to read and write. Literacy in their own language became the goal of many Cherokees. A Constitution was drafted; a newspaper focused on tribal affairs was regularly published. As a literate tribe, Cherokees were vastly superior in communicative skills to most of the whites who were settling Cherokee homeland, now the Southeastern United States.

The vision that Sequoyah had in 1809 grew dim in the America of the late twentieth century. Today twenty percent of our population is functionally illiterate. Half of the occupants of our prisons cannot read or write. The inability of an individual to read or write is an iron door foreclosing his future and dooming him to an undernourished intellectual life.

On the plus side today there is a new Sequoyah,

symbolized by the Literacy Volunteers of America. A legion of 80,000 volunteer tutors are leading their illiterate students to the love of the written word. LVA has corporate sponsors, leaders of industry of the likes of IBM, Gannett, Coors, Motorola and American Express.

Consider this scene observed one day in the Phoenix Public Library. The woman was white, and from her dress, demeanor and personal grooming, was from an upper level of society. The man was black, of modest attire and well past middle age. Together they worked through a book. She helped him sound out the difficult words, and when he pronounced a word on first effort, or speeded his reading of the text, he smiled. Then so did she.

Here was a woman who could have spent the morning in a country club tennis court, or in a luxurious spa. She didn't. She wanted to make some small difference in the world. It was a scene worthy of tears as well as smiles.

Literacy must become the norm in America; illiteracy, an artifact.

In California the Sequoia National Forest is Sequoyah's monument. Perhaps an old black man who sits in the winter sun and reads, will be hers.

Please forgive me. Years ago I was warned that a proper essayist keeps personal pronouns to a minimum. Or better yet, non-existent. But I cannot write this without personal reference.

The winter recital was held at the John Suter Academy of Piano Arts and Science in Prescott Valley. It's an impressive facility, located on the point of a low hill, affording a 270-degree view of the surrounding mountains. The academy houses three Steinway grand pianos, two seven-foot models, circa 1923, and one magnificent nine-foot concert grand, an 1885 instrument, completely restored a century later. This was the Steinway the students used for the recital.

The teacher, Cristina Cuda-Robertson, who presented her students, is a talented pianist with the soul of an artist and the patience a good teacher must possess. Both the selections and the students varied greatly in their musical complexities. The beginner's intense concentration on simple drill was no less impressive than the victory of an intermediate student playing Chopin, Schubert or Liszt with commendable competence.

Fourteen students performed. One was unable to attend. So Steven Campbell, an accomplished pianist, played a Debussy composition which must have inspired every student present. It reminded us that music is a language understood by all peoples.

To me, the piano is the solid skeleton which supports and strengthens the orchestra. If there is royalty among the musical instruments of humankind, the piano is emperor. It has more moods than brass, strings or percussion. It is kind and forgiving to the novice. It challenges the veteran musician. It speaks to all of us.

Sisters, brothers, parents, grandparents, family friends and lovers of children were all in attendance at Mr. Suter's Academy. We were seated on two levels, one by one above the venerable Steinway. The program was arranged on a progressive format, beginning with a dual piano drill, student and teacher, to the advanced student demonstrating evidence of a promising future.

A dear little five-year old was first. He was led to the huge concert grand by his teacher. When he was seated he felt to find the position of the keyboard. Then played the scales, lacking the touch that only time will bring. Neither his parents nor grandparents are musicians. His great-grandmother was, though—a graduate of the Chicago Institute of Music a century ago. She was of concert level. Her family remembers hearing her play *Clair de Lune* late at night when she was troubled and unable to sleep.

When Paul was finished, his teacher took his hand and returned him to his place among the waiting students.

Understand, Paul was born blind.

There was an applause. There were teary cheeks and damp eyes. All of Paul's family was there, mother, father, aunts, cousins, grandparents. His great-grandmother? I am certain she was there also.

© 1994 Bill Ahrendt

CHAPTER 4

Ruff & Ready Remembrances

Lacking both the benefit and handicap of a Harvard Law School education, I am not going to stick my neck out and say that it was the fastest mistrial in Arizona history. But it may well have been. My information came to me from the frequent recital of Judge John J. Hawkins' stories by my father and uncle years ago. My uncle was a territorial sheriff who worked with the judge and admired him greatly.

Hawkins was born in Missouri in 1855. Following graduation from high school, he attended William Jewell College and the University of Missouri. He was admitted to the Missouri Bar in 1878, following which he engaged in private practice in Glasgow, Missouri for five years.

Seduced by romantic tales, young Hawkins headed west and arrived in Prescott, Arizona Territory in November, 1883. Two years later he was chosen probate judge of Yavapai County. Yavapai at the time was the largest county in the territory, bigger than New England, running from just north of Phoenix to the Utah line and west of Holbrook to Kingman. Later, when he left the Yavapai bench, Hawkins served as auditor of the territory. He also was elected a member of the council of the Seventeenth Legislative Assembly. He served on the Territorial Supreme Court from 1893 to 1897.

Judge Hawkins was presiding in the Yavapai County court when the record mistrial took place. A young man was arrested by a deputy sheriff near Kirkland, a small ranching community southwest of Prescott, and charged with a felony. The choreography of the courtroom was strictly observed as it always was when Hawkins presided. When the judge walked toward his bench, the bailiff hammered the gavel and everyone in the courtroom stood. When the judge was seated, the bailiff signaled again. All sat down to begin the process that both sides hoped would end in what they regarded as justice.

One individual remained standing: the young man charged with the crime. He seemed disoriented and confused. Judge Hawkins, obviously annoyed, leaned over and asked the still-standing individual: "Are you the defendant in this case?"

The trial ended abruptly with the blurted response: "No, your honor. I'm the guy that stole the horse!"

Wars, treaties and revolutions have always been the ultimate deciders of the territory of people. The size, scope and to some extent, the character of the American Southwest, was determined by such events.

The Mexican War of 1846-1848 was the initial step of enlarging the size of the American Southwest. The war was not popular. Both the press and the public voiced open opposition to sending U.S. troops onto Mexican soil. The conflict, however, was national policy and the Army used the invasion and resulting combat as a training ground for the Civil War, thought to be inevitable.

Both Robert E. Lee and U.S. Grant were among the young officers who benefitted from the learning experience. While the protest on the home front was as vigorous as the Vietnam demonstrations 125 years later, this war was fought to a successful conclusion.

The Treaty of Guadalupe dramatically changed the face of both Mexico and the United States. Texas had already been lost by Mexico, declaring itself to be an independent republic. The Treaty of Guadalupe, followed four years later by the Gadsden Purchase, resulted in Mexico losing forty percent of its territory and the United States increasing its size by one-third.

New Mexico, Arizona, California, Nevada, Utah, half of Colorado and parts of Wyoming, Kansas and Oklahoma, a domain of more than one million square miles, now comprise a major addition to the United States.

The cost? Thirteen thousand American lives lost by military action and disease, $97 million for the conduct of the war, $29 million paid to Mexico in reparations, and nearly $4 million in claims held by U. S. citizens against Mexico which the United States agreed to pay.

When the cost of human life and *gringo* dollars became public, the "peace at any price" segment of society screamed its outrage. But as time went on, it became clear that the total money price was a bargain. Within two years after the signing of the Treaty of Guadalupe, California, the prize acquisition, had produced as much gold as the entire annexation had cost.

The issue of "freeland"—that in which slavery was forbidden—was hotly debated in and out of Congress. An amendment to an appropriations bill was added by Representative David Wilmot of Pennsylvania, forbidding slavery in any territory acquired from Mexico. Wilmot's amendment was passed by the House but defeated in the Senate.

James Gadsden was the personal representative of President Franklin Pierce empowered to purchase additional territory from Mexico. Gadsden conducted extensive negotiations. One proposal was to include the Mexican states of Coahuila, Chihuahua, Sonora and Baja California. A firm agreement was reached and the international border was to meet the sea eighteen miles south of present-day Guaymas, Sonora. The price, $15 million.

Had the agreement been concluded the American Southwest today would have a seaport enabling world trade. It was not to be. Although it was three decades away, railroad promoters and their lobbyists were planning to extend their rails west to the Pacific. They objected to a seaport in the region they wanted to serve exclusively; sea shipping was much cheaper than rail freight rates.

As is the normal pattern, Congress bowed to those who put money in the basket. Gadsden was ordered to establish the border farther north precluding access to the Sea of Cortez. With no adjustment of the purchase price the border was established as it exists today. The Mexicans did not object to selling less land for the same money.

They were pleased, but confused, by the *gringo* logic. The railroad promoters, aided and abetted by the U. S. Congress, deprived the Southwest of a seaport. It was a selfish, greedy political maneuver which has cost the region dearly.

Wars, treaties and revolutions? Politics, too, determines the size and character of the land on which we dwell.

Now, nearing the end of the twentieth century, perhaps we should look back over those ninety years and the changes they have wrought. The United States Marine Corps is 216 years old today, November 10, 1991, and while proud Maine traditions have remained intact, practices and protocols have kept pace with contemporary technology.

In the field of medicine numerous dread diseases, polio among them, have been controlled or eliminated. Transportation has advanced from the iron tire and oak spoke to a leisurely lunch between London and New York. A menu of eclectic entertainment is at our fingertips.

Outer space has become the new frontier and what once was a golden spike is now called Skylab. Perhaps the miracle of the age occurred on the Moon when an eighteen-handicapper hit a soft six-iron 512 yards, an even 400 yards past my best two-wood.

Sadly, not all elements that make up our life have advanced, refined and moved forward. The once-great American hamburger comes to mind. Cradled within a lightly toasted bun, it was a warm and substantial oval of protein, dressed with crisp lettuce, a juicy slice of garden-ripened tomato and flavor-enhanced by a disk of Vidalia onion and exotic sauces of consumer's choice. Not now.

This once-proud patty of juicy beef has been reduced to a near meatless wafer, precooked, overpriced, devoid of either flavor or character, vacuous, and offering neither nourishment nor gratification.

There is a critical service in our lives that in the past two centuries has made minimal progress. When rummaging through my disheveled files the other day, a copy of a citizen's petition published in a Prescott newspaper of May 23, 1866, got my attention. Among the signers of the complaint were such influential citizens of Prescott as King S. Woolsey, Indian fighter par excellence, who eventually was ambushed by Apaches at Bitter Springs; John H. Marion, editor and tongue-lasher who preceded Jim Garner in this role; R.W. Groom, who surveyed and platted the City of Prescott, an act from which we still suffer; Joseph R. Walker; mountain man and guide, who brought the first twenty-six citizens into Prescott and admonished them to close the gate behind them, a sound warning they chose to ignore. And finally, Lord Darrell Duppa, bon vivant, who obtained infamy as the founder of Phoenix and perpetrator of other atrocities. Their petition was signed and filed with the Postmaster General of the United States. It reads as follows:

> The mail contractor is guilty of gross negligence in his duties; he has failed to deliver our mail with any regularity. He has neglected to comply with the ordinary requirements of mail service. He has been the cause of depriving us of communication with our friends in the East and West, and has interrupted the business intercourse of this community thereby causing the mail to be a detriment rather than a benefit. In proof of this we submit the following affidavits. We earnestly protest against these evils and pray for redress of our grievances...."

The petition was attested to by Acting Governor Richard C. McCormick of the Territory of Arizona. The last I knew, neither Woolsey, Marion, Groom, Walker nor Lord Duppa had heard anything from the Postmaster General, but the letter may be in the mail.

During the Paris revolt of 1848, one of the followers said of a leader, "On the first day of the revolution he was a treasure; on second he ought to be shot."

So it is with revolutions. The Spanish throne ruled Mexico for 281 years. From 1540 until the signing of the Treaty of Córdoba in 1821, the legions of Spain kept the king's cruel claws on the throats of the Mexican people.

Theirs was not a quick revolution. It lasted eleven years and, as is often the case, it created conditions far worse than those it intended to correct. Oppressors are frequently replaced by oppressors. Out of the frying pan and into the fire is a lesson yet to be fully appreciated by revolutionists and reformers. So it was in Mexico.

As with most Mesoamerican revolutions in the past four centuries, the clergy also had a hand in this one. The Mexican priest, Costilla Hidalgo, a tempestuous curate from Durango, tried for years, unsuccessfully, to improve social conditions for his people.

After meeting with failure, time and time again, he resorted to the desperate solution, proclaiming an all-out revolt on September 16, 1810. Hidalgo was joined by Allende and Aldama, semi-soldiers of revolution, and together they seized Guanajuato and Guadalajara. Overly optimistic, because they had captured two cities with so little effort, they marched on the capital of Mexico City with an army of 80,000 ill-trained and undisciplined troops.

The initial assault was successful, but they failed to press the victory by occupying the city. They preferred to remain on the outskirts. Here they built fires and prematurely celebrated victory, roasting meat and drinking mescal. (I know from my field research that this native liquor can impair one's physical and mental capabilities.)

On November 6, 1810, the Spanish Gen. Felix Calleja put the celebrants to rout. Two months later, in

January, 1811, near Guadalajara, Hildalgo's army was annihilated by General Calleja. Father Hidalgo was not among the many combat casualties. And for the next few months he remained a fugitive from Spanish revenge, seeking succor in the homes of Mexican faithful. Somewhere in the North he was betrayed, captured by a Spanish patrol and summarily executed. The fight for Mexico's freedom, however, did not die with Padre Hidalgo.

For the next ten years, Mexico was in fact ruled by two separate governments. At various times, one or another dominated, depending on the locale and the mood of the people. Skirmish after skirmish took place. The revolutionaries, employing guerrilla tactics, endured while the Spanish military grew weak through the ordeal. Three centuries of occupation were coming to an end.

The little wealth Spain drew from this primitive portion of the earth was counterbalanced by a steady cost of suppression. Spain's sea power, once the most formidable in European waters, was threatened. Colonization reduced, rather than replenished, national wealth. Spain decided to withdraw from Mexico.

In 1821, the Treaty of Córdoba was signed by a former Spanish soldier, now a Mexican general, Agustin de Iturbide. Viceroy O'Donoju signed for Spain. Then it began again. General Iturbide became Emperor of Mexico, taking the title Agustin I. A student of Old World rule, he immediately initiated several demonic policies.

These led again to repression, and repression to revolution. Agustin I lasted but a year. On March 19, 1823 he abdicated and was exiled to Europe. His life in a strange land was austere; he was not accorded the courtesies due a crown. Destitute, he returned to Mexico to regain his former power. That was a mistake. Once on Mexican soil he was taken into custody. He died before a firing squad.

Agustin I, the first Emperor of Mexico, became the victim of what he once fought to eliminate. So it is with revolutions.

On the first day of the revolution he was a treasure; on the second...

Richard Elihu Sloan, the last Arizona territorial governor, had just turned twenty-one when he graduated from Monmouth College in Illinois. Footloose and uncertain as to how he would live his life, he went west where the myth of gold and glamour still survived.

Colorado had been admitted to the Union as a state two years before (1876), and Sloan believed it to be Midasland. In retrospect, one would have to question his judgment, for he engaged in mining and newspaper work. Both fields are known as birthing rooms of personal bankruptcy.

He did, however, detect this fatal flaw and enrolled in the Cincinnati School of Law. Upon graduating, Sloan and his friend, L.H. Chalmers, headed west again to establish a law practice. Phoenix was recommended as a fertile field and it was here the law firm of Sloan and Chalmers began.

Legal work proved scarce, so Chalmers joined the firm of Tweed and Hancock, and Sloan accepted the job as district attorney in Florence. He also served a term in the Territorial Legislature and in 1890 was appointed to the Arizona Territorial Supreme Court.

When President Grover Cleveland was elected to a second term in 1892, Judge Sloan lost his seat on the bench. It proved a blessing. The judge had always been fond of Prescott, so he entered private practice here and built a magnificent two-story home on North Mt. Vernon Avenue. It still serves as a church manse. For the next five years, the Sloan family lived here in baronial splendor. The judge hired the finest cook from the Chinese community, an assertive and gifted man named Lng.

John Mason Ross, a Prescott attorney and friend of Judge Sloan, often dined at the Sloan home. He was fond of the Judge's wine selection as well as the products of Lng's kitchen.

In 1897, Judge Sloan was again appointed to the Supreme Court. The territory was now divided into three judicial districts and the judge frequently was required to travel to various locations. On one occasion, the Sloans were to be absent from Prescott for several weeks.

As a gesture of friendship, Sloan lent Lng to Ross for that time. Ross was delighted and hosted a number of dinners, paying Lng well for the additional workload. Ross, however, was in the habit of enjoying a huge breakfast, something Lng deplored and finally refused to furnish. When the Sloan family returned to Prescott they learned of the breakfast battle waged by the two men.

In the kindest of tones, Judge Sloan asked his faithful servant about the problem. Lng, impressed by his employer's judicial position and Lincoln-like physique, explained, "He want bacon, liver, eggs, and biscuits every morning. I no cook. He eat too much he get too fat. Never be a judge, always be a lawyer."

Sloan regarded Lng's answer as one of the finest oral arguments he had ever been privileged to hear. Ross held a different opinion, as attorneys are wont to do.

Shortly after he was inaugurated, President William Howard Taft summoned Judge Sloan to the White House. Taft appointed Sloan governor of the Territory of Arizona.

Mayor Morris Goldwater introduced the governor to a capacity crowd at the Prescott Opera House. His message was clear. He would work for statehood and reclamation for Arizona. Following the governor's talk, Prescott celebrated. Both newspapers mentioned the festive mood of the populace which lasted through the night.

The parting of Sloan and Prescott was sad. The lovely home was sold and the family moved to the capital city of Phoenix just in time to face the non-air-conditioned summer of 1909. In his memoirs, Judge Sloan tells of the brutal heat of a Phoenix summer sans coolers.

As governor, he was to inspect the enlarging of the Arizona Canal. It was being excavated by shovel in midsummer by men on twelve-hour work shifts. On the bank of the canal he saw a simple wooden hand-carved headboard, which marked the grave of one of the laborers. Its message, Governor Sloan never forgot.

Here lies John Coil,
A son of toil.
He died right here,
On Arizona soil.
He was a man of considerable vim.
But this here air was too hot for him.

The image of frontier justice has been unfairly dealt with in fiction. The typical judge of the Old West was pictured as a semi-skilled boozer, short on law and patience. All too often he was described as barely literate. His chin would be stained with tobacco juice, his vest with gravy. Such was not the case of Horace B. Roby.

A native of Vermont, Roby before the Civil War had practiced law in Rutland, where he was the local power broker for the Republican Party. Commissioned a major at the outbreak of the war, he served on the staff of General Grant in the final months of that tragic affair. Retiring a full colonel, he wandered west to reestablish his career and satisfy his newly acquired taste for excitement. Roby was living in Nevada in 1868 when then-President Grant asked him to serve as judge of the Second Judicial District of the Territory of Arizona.

In 1872 Mohave and Yuma counties comprised the court district over which Judge Roby presided. He lived in Yuma, sharing a well-ordered house with his wife and two small children. Even in the cruel desert heat of a Yuma summer, the judge wore his striped woolen trousers, black broadcloth coat and silk hat. He shunned the local spas, returning daily to his home library where he pursued the honing of his scholarship and a quiet family life. Only an occasional trip to the county seat of Mohave County interrupted his pleasant routine. The county seat, Hardyville, on the muddy Colorado River, was not his favorite judicial retreat.

Early in 1872, Judge Roby was called to Hardyville to hear a murder case. A local miner was accused of killing a soldier in a military-industrial confrontation at a local bar. The judge booked passage on a stern-wheeler riverboat and headed upriver. He was aware of the limited facilities, and, as in previous visits, arranged to sleep in a rear alcove of Hardy's Saloon. His meals were available at Wooster Hardy's dining room. Many miners and freighters in town for the trial cooked over open fires and slept on the desert floor. The judge was fortunate to have a roof overhead.

On the second night of the trial, witnesses, miners, soldiers, attorneys and clerks in service to the court all were celebrating in the saloon where in the rear alcove Judge Roby was trying to get a night's rest.

After futilely seeking slumber for half the night, the judge arose, went to the rear of the saloon and demanded the sheriff bring the prisoner. The sheriff, seated in a chair tilted against the wall, was found to be incapable of following the judge's order. A deputy was dispatched to bring forth the prisoner. Judge Roby, now seated in back of the bar, opened Arizona's first night court. Witnesses were called, testimony heard, and by dawn the jury retired to reach a verdict.

The smell and sound of bacon and eggs frying must have aided the jury in reaching a verdict. The judge asked each man who thought the miner innocent of killing the soldier, to place his hat on the bar when he reentered the saloon. All hats soon covered the bar.

After breakfast the judge declared the defendant free to go and suggested that the verdict might well be a declaration of open season on soldiers. He then sent a message to the riverboat captain, who was about to depart, to wait until he was aboard.

Then Judge Roby addressed the citizens of Hardyville. He informed them that if Mohave County desired the services of the court, it had better provide adequate facilities in the near future. Then, briefcase in hand, Judge Roby caught the boat to his comfortable home in Yuma. The first night court in Arizona adjourned *sine die.*

On that "day in infamy," a young boy stood on the slope of Diamond Head and watched as the *USS Arizona* settled into the muddy bottom of

Pearl Harbor, leaving only a plume of smoke like a rose on a casket.

Forty-one years later, Cecil Gates built a thirty-four foot replica of the *Arizona,* entered it in the Fiesta Bowl parade and afterward gave it to the State of Arizona.

I learned of another *Arizona* when I was a guest at a party in Santa Fe, New Mexico, home several years ago. My host, knowing of my origins, took me to his dining room and proudly pointed to an oil painting of the first *Arizona* his great-grandfather served on as a young officer.

I had always presumed there was but one *Arizona.* Now I know there were three, perhaps four, depending on how you calculate. My host, an expert on the subject, recited the history.

The first *Arizona* was built in Wilmington, Delaware, in 1858. At the time she was commissioned, Arizona as such did not exist. The name was used only as a vague reference to the western half of the then New Mexico Territory. Not until President Lincoln created the Territory of Arizona in 1863, did Arizona become an official entity.

The first *Arizona* was an ironclad paddle-wheel steamer. She was lightly armed and placed in U.S. Navy service where she was assigned to coastal patrol during the uneasy days just before the firing on Fort Sumter.

When the War Between the States began in earnest, she was captured by the Confederate Navy. Rebels changed her name to *Caroline* and put her in service running the federal blockade along the Gulf Coast. In October, 1862 she was in Havana harbor in command of Captain Lyman Redford of the Confederate Navy.

The Confederate blockade runners were, in effect, privateers. The crew, captain and ship owners were paid by the Confederacy on the basis of the contraband they managed to deliver to Confederate ports. (You may recall the character Rhett Butler in the novel and film, *Gone With the Wind.*)

Mobile, Biloxi and New Orleans were the favorite terminal ports. When Captain Redford left Havana harbor he set a zigzag course in hopes of reaching Mobile, Alabama. He had in the hold 1,500 gallons of Cuban rum, cane sugar and materiel of war: guns, ammunition, wagons, harness, and more.

On October 28, 1862, in sight of the Alabama coast, the Union warship *Montgomery* captured the *Caroline*, her crew and cargo. The *Caroline* was taken to Philadelphia for a major overhaul. Here she was painted, refitted and supplied. Her firepower and armor were greatly increased.

Emerging like new from refitting, the *Caroline* again became the *Arizona*, assigned to blockade Confederate ports. In December, 1864, with New Orleans under federal control, the *USS Arizona* was cautiously moving up the Mississippi estuary to New Orleans.

She bristled with a battery of eight guns and carried a crew of ninety-eight when she was attacked by a small, makeshift Confederate vessel. A lucky shot from the enemy hit the *Arizona* midship and set her afire. Four of her crew were killed and the remainder abandoned ship as the flames ate at her hull. She sank below the surface into the ooze of the Mississippi River.

Two other *Arizonas* followed her in service. The last one now rests in Pearl Harbor and serves as a crypt for the men who died with her. Someday perhaps, another *USS Arizona* will sail the seas of the world as a peacekeeper with a heroic, historic name.

He was born with the most conspicuous of birthmarks — a famous father. That burden however, did not deter Sam Houston's youngest son of his own growth and development and the self-assurance that comes with success. Temple Houston was born in the critical year of 1860. His father was governor of Texas at the time and resigned a year later because he would not sign allegiance to the Confederacy. Thirty-five years earlier he had resigned as governor of Tennessee. Temple, who was only three when his father died, was fond of saying that his father resigned as governor of Tennessee because of the love of a woman and of Texas because of the love of his country.

As a youth, Temple worked as a page in both the Texas Legislature and the United States Congress. In both jobs he studied law. The many stories that have generated regarding his gunfights mingle fact and folklore, but the stories of his highly charged emotional speeches to the jury, are for the most part, documented by court record.

In 1890, in Woodward, Oklahoma, where he had moved only a year before, he was asked to defend Minnie Stacey. Minnie had been charged with prostitution, and several of Woodward's leading citizens were trying to have her sent to the territorial prison. In one of his most dramatic charges, Temple Houston in swallow-tailed coat and high black boots, pleaded for mercy.

"Let us judge her gently. Only a moment ago the prosecutors reproached her for the depths to which she has sunk, the company she has kept, the life she has led. Now what is left to her? Where can she go that sin does not pursue her? Society has reared relentless walls around her. You know the story of the Prodigal Son. Yet, for the Prodigal Daughter there is no return.

"The Master, while on this earth, spake with wrath and rebuke to kings and rulers. He never reproached a woman such as we see here today. One he forgave. Another he acquitted. You remember both. And now, looking on this friendless outcast, can any of us say to her, 'I am holier than thou!'

"Those who brought the woman before the Savior have been held up to the contempt of the world for two thousand years. I have always respected them. Men who yield to the reproaches of conscience, as they did, have elements of good in them. If the prosecutors of this woman, whom this court is trying, had brought her before the Savior, they would have accepted His challenge, and each would have picked up a rock and stoned her in a twinkling of an eye.

"No, gentlemen of the jury, do as your Master did twice in the very same circumstances that now surround you.

"Tell her to go and sin no more.

"Tell her to go in peace."

Minnie Stacey was acquitted by the first vote of the jury. It has been said that the experience changed her life. She became a nurse, married and lived an exemplary life in Amarillo, Texas. Temple Houston died in bed of pneumonia when only forty-five years of age. To the end he revered his father and family. An old friend of the family who, though in his eighties, still practiced law in Austin, closed his office and spoke at the funeral. He paid a great tribute when he said,"You could count on Temple Houston. Temple would have charged Hell with only one bucket of water."

As he sat in his small cell and listened to the sounds of the Army carpenters constructing his gallows, he made a decision. Samuel H. Calhoun, age twenty-two, requested permission from his jailer to see Capt. Jonathan H. Greene, a writer. To Greene he told his story. The confession given in Bardstown, Kentucky on February 3, 1862, added a violent and unknown chapter to the history of Arizona.

Greene was a good listener and skilled notetaker. In the few remaining hours left, he outlined the tragic life of Calhoun. A tiny book, published later that year in Cincinnati in limited edition, documented the two years Calhoun had spent in Southern Arizona as a bullion messenger, Indian fighter and desperado. His candid confession of his many vicious slayings of man and animal leaves little doubt about the justice of his final destiny.

Calhoun was born in Virginia in 1839, and orphaned at an early age. His foster parents were kind and gentle folk doing the best they could to raise a rebellious youth. Sam ran away to Baltimore at the age of eleven, where he was taken in tow by a traveling huckster and counterfeiter.

Quickly learning the art of lawless survival, he took passage to New Orleans, where he became the leader of a gang that stole goods from the docks and fenced them to merchants indifferent to the source of supply. When he became aware of a trap being set by the New Orleans police, he directed his gang into it, and absconded with their shares of previous operations.

With the freedom of wealth, needing a veil of respectability, he journeyed to Texas and joined the newly formed Texas Rangers to fight Indians. His unbounded enthusiasm for the wanton killing of "savages," using his bowie knife with neurotic devotion, caused his comrades to question his stability. They were sickened by his delight in what they considered an unpleasant task. In 1858, no longer welcome as a Texas Ranger, he wandered west.

Somewhere in Southern New Mexico, Sam Calhoun became the uninvited guest of an immigrant train heading toward Arizona. The party experienced a normal amount of Indian confrontations en route and lost several mules to the hungry Apaches. Calhoun decided to leave the group near Tucson upon hearing of employment openings at the Patagonia Mines on the Mexican border. Here he found work as a bullion messenger and mine guard, transporting pure silver ore to Mexico city to trade for gold coins.

After delivery of the Patagonia ore, he remained in Mexico City for several days, prowling the city alone to savor the sights. Spotting two raucous *ricos* on a deserted street, he killed the pair with his bowie knife and stripped the bodies of valuables. Shedding his guilt as a snake would its skin, he returned to the mines.

A few days after Calhoun's arrival in Patagonia, several Mexican bandits raided the camp in the dead of night, killing two of the guards, and rode off with eight mules and nineteen horses. The following morning, at the request of the mine manager, Calhoun took four guards and three Apache guides in pursuit of the raiders. On the third day out, in the Yaqui River Valley, the search party spotted the bandit camp.

After dark, when all was quiet, they infiltrated the camp using the best guerrilla stealth, and murdered the bandits in their bedrolls. At dawn the Calhoun party took a quick inventory, discovered to their delight nearly a hundred horses and mules, more than forty head of cattle, several woolen rebozos and other Mexican merchandise. Calhoun and the guards killed the Apache scouts and headed south with their booty.

Several days later, they arrived at an imposing

hacienda and trading post where they sold their ill-gotten gains for $6,000. Calhoun assured the guards he would divide the money when they arrived in Mexico City. Early one morning a few miles north of the capital, the four sleepy guards found Calhoun's bedroll empty. Before they could overtake him, Calhoun was well on his way to the port of Veracruz.

Calhoun stayed in Veracruz for several months, living a quiet but comfortable life. On his twenty-first birthday in 1860, he took passage on a ship to New Orleans, his bloody adventures in the Southwest concluded.

In New Orleans it was obvious a Civil War would soon divide a great nation. Feeling an uncharacteristic surge of patriotism, Calhoun caught a river boat from New Orleans to Cincinnati, where he enlisted in the Second Kentucky Regiment of the Union Army. A year later, stationed near Bardstown, Kentucky, Pvt. Samuel H. Calhoun killed a farmer after stealing a hog from his farm.

The court-martial took two days. He was executed February 5, 1862. Because of the demands of justice, a shameful chapter of Arizona history saw the light of publication. The original text is still available on microfilm at the Historical Society of Pennsylvania.

The case centered on the sometimes stream of Kirkland Creek in southwest Yavapai County. The tragic drama it created was announced to the community when a frightened spectator ran out of the courthouse and shouted, "They're killing people like sheep up there."

Kelsey vs. McAteer et al.
Water rights on Kirkland Creek.
Yavapai County, Arizona. December 2, 1883
Prescott, Arizona Territory.

Moses Langley originally was listed as a defendant. But the case was being retried and Langley was on the stand this cold December afternoon testifying for the plaintiff. The 300-pound judge C.G.W. French was robed and ready for the afternoon session, but a bit logy from a huge pork noodle lunch.

C.B. Rush, attorney for the defendants, was also the county attorney and on cross examination pointed out an affidavit Langley had made in the earlier 1878 trial. It differed, he said, from the testimony Langley had just given. Clark Churchill, attorney for the plaintiff and attorney general for the territory, on direct examination, offered to introduce the entire affidavit. Rush objected. Churchill, in a strong Shakespearian voice, declared that Rush had garbled the affidavit. That lit the fuse.

Rush shouted, "Mr. Churchill, you dare not charge me with garbling an instrument!"

Churchill replied, "If you say you did not garble the affidavit, you lie." Churchill then threw an ink well at Rush striking him in the throat. Rush replied by imbedding his fist into Churchill's face. As Churchill and Rush fell upon one another *mano a mano*, J.C. Herndon, Rush's assistant, hurled another ink well into the face of the attorney general. Then the defendant, Patrick McAteer, entered the fray. James More, one of the defendants, and Charles Beach, who was married to a Kelsey daughter, landed telling blows on Rush. McAteer produced a sizable knife and tried to stab Attorney General Churchill. Buckey O'Neill, the court reporter, dived toward McAteer. McAteer's knife ended up deep in the shoulder of James More, then again in the neck of Charles Beach who fell into the spectators section. His knife still in hand, McAteer headed for Buckey. Beach, now bleeding profusely, drew a revolver from his belt and fired. McAteer fell at O'Neill's feet.

A deputy sheriff released all the prisoners from their cells and led them into the courtroom to stop the slaughter. Amid moans and groans, the fighting ceased. Chief Justice French was found in the corner of the courtroom under a pile of chairs, his pork noodle lunch now knotted in his stomach, his gavel still in hand.

James More died a few days following the amputation of his arm. Charles Beach retired to his residence where his physician dressed his wounds. Buckey O'Neill and Attorney General Churchill were treated at the Sisters' Hospital. Chief Justice French fined both Rush and Churchill $500 for contempt of court and cut in half the remaining time of the prisoners who restored law and order to the courtroom. Chief Justice French then released a statement to the *Prescott Courier.* It was a classic fantasy: "Had it not been for my coolness and presence of mind, more people would have been killed or injured."

Today our attorneys don't throw inkwells—but they still throw ink well words.

The award-winning epic film, *Dances with Wolves,* has a generic quality to it, reminding me of incidents in frontier history where adversaries became allies. While this excellent film was pure fiction, two close cousins of *Dances with Wolves* come to mind. Both are factual. Both have been studied and written about by military historians, distinguished academicians and hopeless romantics: Evan Connell, Odie Faulk and myself.

In 1878, marauding Apaches became an ever-increasing security threat along the Arizona-Mexican border. Army troops stationed at Camp Supply in the Pedregosa Mountains, due east of Tombstone, seemed incapable of keeping the Apaches in check.

A recent West Point graduate, Lt. Austin Henely, convinced his commanding officer that with forty Indian scouts and three or four enlisted men, he could bring peace to the borderlands.

The commanding officer, skeptical but desperate, granted permission for an independent unit to roam the countryside at will. To give the group mobility, the scouts suggested an Indian diet of dried meat, beans and the native liquor, tiswin. The meat and beans would furnish nourishment, the tiswin, courage and composure.

Living daily with his Indians, Lieutenant Henely adapted to their ways. He learned their language, ate their food and drank their liquor. He added a few ceremonial feathers to his brass buttons.

He replaced his gold bars with colorful ribbons. For four years, Austin Henely and his special detail patrolled the borderland. They suffered some losses in tribal combat, a few desertions and some accidental deaths. A part-time peace came in 1882, and Henely, having no desire to return to a monotonous garrison life, asked to be dismissed from service.

When Austin Henely rode out of Fort Rucker in the southeast section of the Arizona Territory in the autumn of 1882, his long hair was tied with a band. Ceremonial festoons flowed from the shoulders of his Army jacket. He wore a breech cloth over a G-string and knee-high Apache moccasins with silver buttons. Besides his Army jacket, his only other remnant of military life was his McClellan saddle. History hasn't heard from him since.

While the fact, fiction and folklore regarding Lt. Henely is atypical for a West Point graduate, that of the cadet Henry McLean is even more so. He was appointed to the United States Military Academy in 1844. He was from a prominent Missouri family and a nephew of Senator John McLean of Illinois.

He was a man of medium height with a large head, bushy uncombed hair, bull neck and massive shoulders. Hence his West Point nickname, Bison. In his four years at the Academy, he seemed antisocial and reclusive; yet he would leave the campus at times to visit a girl friend in Buttermilk Falls, a nearby village. A few days before he was to graduate, Cadet McLean imbibed at the village bar and got into a fight. He beat his opponent nearly to death.

This indiscretion resulted in the withholding of his commission. Furious, the young man walked off the pages of history and into the fuzzy world of folklore. What happened to Bison after he left school has been the product of a hundred pens and as many imaginative minds. If the truth ever comes to the printed page, it might be one of the following scenarios subscribed to by many.

- After wandering around the West for several years, he lived out his life as a half-animal on the estuary where the Colorado River joins the Sea of Cortez. This is a favorite legend of Mexican fisherman.
- In another yarn, Bison met his end at the hands of the Apaches near Tubac, Arizona Territory.
- In yet another version, a classmate claimed he met Bison in 1852 in New Mexico. Bison was living in a pueblo village. He had been arrested in Galveston, Texas, when he got into a brawl with some ships' officers.
- Another tale holds that the brilliant Indian military strategist, Sitting Bull, was in fact, Bison, a gifted student of tactics.

• This one is my favorite. In 1858, Lt. Joseph C. Ives of the U.S. Army Topographical Engineers, was surveying the Colorado River when a group of Mojaves approached the survey party. They spoke in Spanish and communication was difficult. Then the Mojave leader asked in excellent French, then English: "Ives, don't you know me?"

Lt. Ives, somewhat shocked, asked, "Where did you learn to speak French and English?" The answer: "Ives, we were cadets together. My Mojaves wanted to attack your party. I would not permit it."

Lt. Ives only stared at the beefy brown figure of a man. Then the Mojaves moved into the river willows on the far bank and disappeared. A voice was heard. "Goodbye, Ives. God bless you."

Cadet McLean, seaport pirate? Sioux chief? River recluse? Killed at Tubac? Mohave? As yet Bison's footprints have never been found.

His memorial is a simple one for a man of his stature. It is a usually dry wash in the high desert country of Northern Arizona. Hamblin Wash heads on the south slope of the Kaibito Plateau northwest of Tuba City and flows south. U.S. Route 160 crosses Hamblin Wash just east of the U.S. 89-U.S. 160 junction a few miles north of Cameron. From here it wanders into the desert, becomes undefined and dies of dehydration in the sands of the Moenkopi Plateau.

A trusted colonizer for Brigham Young, Jacob Hamblin was a quiet, taciturn man who lived by the tenets of The Church of Jesus Christ of Latter-day Saints, but was seldom sheltered by its structure. As early as 1857 he was selected by Young to guide an immigrant party of non-Mormons across Utah to California.

The Mountain Meadows Massacre of a wagon train, by rogue Mormons, was still bitter bile in the mouth of Brigham Young. He wanted assurance that his non-Mormon brothers would pass in peace, unmolested. Hamblin, Young knew, possessed the skills of firm diplomacy to provide that safe conduct.

Hamblin also was a missionary to the Navajos and the Hopis. He was trusted by both tribes in secular affairs, but rejected by the Hopis in theological matters. The Navajos, much less resistant, were curious, but uncommitted when Hamblin told them of his faith and invited them to share it.

When the Grand Canyon explorer, Maj. John W. Powell, needed a competent man to guide him on his travels to the remote areas of the Southwest, he selected Hamblin. His knowledge of the country and his ability to deal peacefully with the Indians were the rare qualities Powell sought. In a book later Powell spoke of him:

> *This man Hamblin speaks the Navajo language well and has a great influence over all Indians round about. He is a silent, reserved man and when he speaks it is in a slow quiet way that inspires great awe. His talk is so low that they must listen attentively to hear, and they sit around him in death-like silence.*

History records but one unpleasant confrontation between Hamblin and the Navajos. Early in 1868 four Navajos were ambushed near Tonalea (Red Lake). Three of the Navajos were killed. One escaped. Jacob Hamblin and two other Mormon men were brought before a Navajo tribunal conducted in a hogan and presided over by twenty-three Navajo braves.

The Navajos sat in a circle around the cedar and mud walls of the shelter. Hamblin and his two fellow missionaries were required to stand in the center during the entire eleven-hour ordeal. If found guilty, death on a bed of coals awaited them. The one surviving Navajo was called to show his wounds and tell of the ambush. The Navajos took turns roaring their accusations and proclaiming the guilt of the Mormons.

All through the protracted procedure, Hamblin stood stoic, unafraid and attentive, respecting the inquiry. Then, as the charges dwindled, he asked to speak. In his usual collected manner, he formed his reply. He reminded them that he had never breached their trust. Deception or violence had never been tools of his mission. With a stick he drew a map of his whereabouts when the attack occurred.

Never having raised his voice or lost his composure, he concluded, expressing faith in universal justice. Serene and assured of here or hereafter, the three Mormon men awaited the verdict. Fire or freedom? In the end, they were told to go in peace.

Jacob Hamblin died on August 31, 1886. His conduct, character and personal integrity made him more than just a hero of his church. He was one of the most productive pioneers in the settling of the Southwest.

Hamblin Wash is a most appropriate memorial. Like the man himself, it too, carries the occasional transfusions which sustain and enrich our lives.

Several years ago in Fort Worth the Texas writer, Elmer Kelton, told me about it. He had written a book on the subject, titled, *The Day the Cowboys Quit.*

It began on the bank of Frio Creek in Deaf Smith County, Texas, March 24, 1883. The ringleader of what would become known as the "Great American Cowboy Strike" was Tom Harris, wagon boss of the LS Ranch.

Harris and five other cowboys from five other ranches drafted the demands, and another cowboy named McClain delivered the strike notices to cowboys on scattered ranches. The strike was set for March 31 and on that historic date about 380 working cowboys on the grasslands of the Panhandle of Texas, "went out."

The monetary demands of the strikers were modest even by the standards of the time. No cowboy was to be paid less than $50 a month. A good cook was to be paid the same. The rancher committee had no problem with the wage scale. What did cause them great concern was the cowboy demand for the right to "maverick"... the privilege to claim any unbranded cattle in order to start small herds of their own.

The ranchers saw a serious threat in the practice of "mavericking." Beyond the loss of a few unbranded cattle they feared the loss of a good cowboy and above all, the loss of the grasslands, bit by bit, piece by piece, as more and more cowboys gained their own herds.

Labor and management tried to resolve the differences. Tom Harris met with W.M.D. Lee and John M. Gist, both prominent Panhandle ranchers. Lee, who employed Harris, studied the demands and offered Harris a steady job at $100 a month. He also agreed to pay any cowboy $50 a month if Harris deemed he was worth it. Both Lee and Gist declared that they would never tolerate "mavericking." Harris rejected the offer and the strike was on.

Texas newspapers generally ignored the cowboy strike and as a result, information is difficult to come by. This editorial snobbery resulted in several independent publications being devoted to the livestock industry, some of which are still alive and prospering.

Like many strikes this one was neither pleasant nor successful. For more than a year the cowboys camped near the tiny town of Tascosa on the Canadian River north of present day Amarillo. They lived on stolen beef, bacon, beans and Arbuckle's coffee.

The labor leader, Tom Harris, deserted early, moved across the line, and being a master at mavericking, went into business for himself in New Mexico Territory. With his ability to find unbranded cattle and his talent with a long rope and a running iron, Tom Harris established his own herd and built up one of the finest ranches in Southeastern New Mexico.

Appropriately, he named it the Get Even Cattle Company.

Fort Whipple and Prescott have been symbiotic neighbors since 1864. During this time, as Whipple evolved from a military installation to public facility and finally Veterans Administration Hospital, it has enriched local history with a constant flow of famous and near famous. Indian Fighter Gen. George Crook; the bandmaster's son, Fiorello La Guardia; Maj. Henry Martyn Robert, who while stationed here wrote the original draft of *Robert's Rules of Order;* and Elliot Coues, Army surgeon and naturalist, generally regarded as the foremost ornithologist of the nineteenth century—all came to the fort on Granite Creek and lived a portion of their lives in the Prescott area.

Of the parade of personalities who have walked along the creek bank from barracks to barroom and back again, none is more interesting than Coues. Born in New Hampshire, Coues moved with his family to Washington D.C., when he was eleven years old. Intrigued with bird life since he was a child, Coues turned to serious study when in Washington at the Smithsonian. Awarded a master's degree in 1862, he enrolled as a medical cadet that same year and graduated a year later as a physician. Only twenty-one years of age, he treated wounded Civil War soldiers at Mount Pleasant Hospital, outside of Washington. In early 1864, Coues was commissioned as a first lieutenant-assistant surgeon.

A common Army practice at the time was to send young, inexperienced medics to distant frontier posts. The policy proved a blessing for young Coues. For during the year he cared for wounded soldiers, he had become intimately involved with an attractive Washington belle. The result was pregnancy and a strong suggestion from members of her family that a wedding would be an appropriate ceremony. Coues agreed, providing he could obtain a divorce after he had arrived at his new post in the Southwest. The wedding was privately performed on the evening of April 24, 1864, in Columbus, Ohio. To avoid any claim that the marriage had been consummated, Coues left his bride and, accompanied by a witness, took a train to Chicago at four in the morning.

His Washington tryst seemed to establish a lifelong pattern of amorous conquest, proving again the validity of the Latin phrase, *amantes sunt amentes*—lovers are lunatics.

When Coues arrived in Santa Fe, General Carleton assigned him to Fort Whipple as medical officer and naturalist. Coues joined a military column a few miles south of Albuquerque, New Mexico. The column consisted of eighty wagons loaded with ordnance and military stores and twelve luggage wagons carrying personal property. Three hundred beeves, 800 sheep and 560 mules moved with the column. One hundred sixty-three cavalrymen protected the train.

On June 16, 1864, the group left the Rio Grande River. En route to Whipple they drove off three Indian attacks, but this danger never deterred Dr. Coues from many side trips to collect specimens. Coues did not limit his collecting to birds. All kinds of zoological specimens were gathered for the Smithsonian Institution. In one wagon he had a five-gallon keg of alcohol in which he pickled various reptiles.

Some of the soldiers, detecting the odor of alcohol, filled their canteens from the keg. They were joyfully celebrating when the keg was brought before them and the top removed. What they saw soon stopped the celebration and induced instant catharsis.

Coues reached Fort Whipple on July 29. He remained only fifteen months. Within a matter of two weeks after his arrival he had the post hospital set up and functioning with the assistance of one orderly. Coues' journals tell of numerous conflicts between Indians and whites. Savage, sadistic warfare saddened him. He blamed both sides for the cruel suffering.

Despite constant danger, Coues went to the field daily to study and collect. He traveled from Prescott for miles in every direction, Bill Williams Mountain and the Verde Valley being favorite haunts. He also ran ads in the newly established Prescott paper stating that he was available to tend to the medical needs of Prescott people, specializing in surgery. By 1866, he was back in Washington, D.C. at the Smithsonian, well on his way to becoming America's foremost ornithologist.

However, before he left Prescott, he lobbied Arizona's first legislature, presenting a memorial and petition, "For the benefit of Elliot Coues." The measure was quickly passed, dissolving bonds of matrimony that had been required by the pregnancy of Sarah. She had suffered a miscarriage, and while that and the Arizona divorce ended the affair, it did little to discourage Elliot's many other amours during his lifetime.

Forty years after Coronado's exploration of what is today the American Southwest, two other Spanish explorers came north from Mexico in search of the fabled Cíbola. They were drawn by rumors of great riches and red-skinned natives awaiting the blessing of Christianity.

Now there was a new fable. Much to the dismay of the Spanish, the English navigator, Sir Francis Drake, had sailed up the west coasts of South, Central and North America, planted the Union Jack, named California, "New Albion," claimed it for his sponsor, Queen Elizabeth I, and disappeared over the horizon.

When reports of Drake's travels reached the Spanish conquistadors in Mexico City the rumor was born. There indeed must be a short cut between the Atlantic and the Pacific. Drake, Spain's bitter foe, had discovered the mythical Strait of Anian?

The Spanish military placed this fabled passage between the seas somewhere north of Mexico, a huge and rather obscure area. The Spanish Crown issued orders to find the Strait of Anian and somehow prevent its use to all ships but those of Spain.

The first foolish probe to find the Strait of Anian was led by a Franciscan friar, Augustin Rodríquez, who headed north on June 5, 1581. His small expedition hoped to find and control the fabled strait, capture the riches of the area and convert the heathen natives.

Arriving at Tiquex, an Indian pueblo just north of present day Albuquerque, they established a base camp. They probed east, then west; no sea in sight. Riches consisted of squash and melons. The Indians of Cíbola expressed complete satisfaction with their own religious practices.

Feeling the thorn of defeat, the military arm of the expedition suggested it was time to return to Mexico.

Rodríquez and two other friars refused to leave, saying they must stay and convert Indians. They remained, never to be seen by their countrymen again.

Two years later in February, came the urbane patron António de Espejo, in search of wealth, converts and the link between the seas. For eight months Espejo searched the area and concluded there was no Strait of Anian in what he named *Nuevo Mexico*.

The Rio Grande, willing as it was, could not meet the needs of the Spanish Armada. While Espejo's stay was brief he was by far the most thorough in his search. He came the closest of all early Spaniards to present-day Prescott. He entered the Verde Valley and reported rich copper deposits, crossed the west end of Mingus Mountain and probably went as far west as Williamson Valley.

As soon as Espejo returned to Mexico, he sailed for Spain to request from the Crown permission and funds to colonize *Nuevo Mexico* extensively, but he died en route and was buried at sea. Because of his exploration of the Prescott area I have always hoped that some quality real estate development would take the name Espejo Estates.

The wealth that Spain envisioned north of Mexico was not to be found. The fabled Seven Cities of Cíbola were nothing more than mud villages. There was no El Dorado or mountain of gold. The Strait of Anian is yet to be discovered. There is however, an American Southwest and for those of us who live here, this is heaven enough.

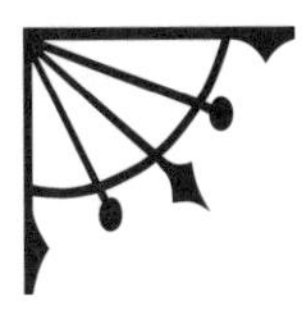

CHAPTER

Ruff Spots of Society

Keep in mind, I am a layman. The man who was to become my father-in-law was an opinionated old goat who insisted I sign a prenuptial agreement never to go to law school. Because of this void in my life, I lack the analytical legal eye to understand the multiple mysteries attorneys must deal with on a daily basis.

Recently I was involved in the maze of an estate being probated. As I observed the process from the sidelines, my memory returned me to a simpler, more basic time and place. The first "probate" I observed differed in a number of ways from the modern one. A half century separated the two. The settings were different. Outdoors—indoors.

The first probate is now ancient history. It was held in a roundup camp sixty-five miles by dirt road from the county seat. The venue was a bosque of cedars, a chuck wagon and a wide ring of bedrolls surrounding it. No noise, save the popping of a wood fire and the low, slow mumbling of men tired from a long day's work.

I arrived at camp with a deputy sheriff who was to investigate the death of a cowboy who "didn't eat no supper" and "just laid down and died." The deputy pulled the tarp back, examined the body from the neck up and came to the speedy but accurate conclusion that death occurred from natural causes. Members of the coroner's jury, of which I was one, nodded in accord.

The wagon-boss told the deputy that the deceased, Buster, had no living kin except a nephew, "counting Sundays" in a Texas prison. The decision was then made that Buster be buried in a secondary cemetery near the county seat. The final tribute would be plain vanilla but would involve a tolerant clergyman if one could be found. The undertaker estimated that about $250 would be required to rotate Buster to a better range. The probate began.

"Does anyone here owe Buster any money?" the deputy asked.

None.

On the asset side, $22 was found in Buster's chaps pocket. One waddy offered to buy the chaps for $30. The liquidation was under way. Buster's N. Porter saddle was on a Port Parker tree and had tooled fenders. It brought $85 from the wagon-boss. Nobody wanted the bedroll but the tarp was bought by the cook for $16.

Buster's split-eared bridle was a beauty. It had a Navajo concha on each cheek strap and the bit was engraved. After obtaining financing, a newly married cowboy bought it for $32. A search of Buster's warbag produced nothing but some toilet articles, an unopened pint of whiskey and a pocket-sized Bible. This was too personal to purchase. It was decided to send the warbag and its contents to be buried with its owner. A pair of California-style spurs and a fine reata brought $38.

When the boss pulled into camp in his pickup, the deputy had $223 cash. On the chuck wagon table in the hissing light of Coleman lantern, the boss counted out enough dollars to assure that when Buster went over the fence line, he owed no man or mortuary.

This cow camp probate took about a half hour.

The indoor probate I mentioned is having a longer run than *My Fair Lady.*

I bought one of those little seventy-five cent appointment books the other day. It cost me $4. It had those little squares that you write in to remind you what you are supposed to do, where you are suppose to go, and when.

While I am sure that will prove helpful, it contains some additional information that I am having a difficult time using.

Decimal equivalents, for example, are of little use to me with the possible exception of balancing my check book. It also has a list of what are called interesting facts. However, I have lost little sleep reading them in bed. One of these blandly stated facts says, "One cubic foot of anthracite coal weighs about fifty-eight pounds." I tried to impress a good-looking widow at a cocktail party the other evening and mentioned that fact to her. She went home alone shortly afterwards.

This little brown book also gives the important days that are to be observed each month. I had no idea how many worthy holidays have gone unobserved and uncelebrated. I can tell you right now that Martin Luther King isn't the only event or individual who has been bypassed (now observed) in Arizona. Just take the month of June for example.

June is Adopt-a-Cat-Month and also Fight-the Filthy-Fly-Month. I have no problem about fighting flies, but I am a little hesitant about adopting a cat. Cats are kind of like quiche. If you have had one once, that's about all you will ever need. June 4 is supposed to be Old Maids Day. I didn't know that there were any old maids left. Now we call them career women. June 9 is Senior Citizen's Day in Oklahoma. I have been to Oklahoma and I don't think that there is a Junior Citizen in the whole damn state. I really like the basic idea behind Blame-Somebody-Else-Day that they celebrate on June 13 in Clio, Michigan. The Edsel automobile no doubt prompted this idea. This is a lesson we all learn very quickly—place the blame on someone else.

You are never going to believe me when I tell you that on June 14 Dairy Goat Awareness Week begins in of all places, Scottsdale, Arizona. I will admit that I have been somewhat unaware of dairy goats. In fact, I have been oblivious to dairy goats. In all fairness, however, I do feel that I can live a good full life without ever giving a dairy goat the time of day.

On June 17 the National Association of Left-Handed Golfers meets in Houston. Golf is a wicked game. Everyone who takes up the game does one of three things: becomes a born-again Christian, starts beating the spouse, (men use their fist, women use a three-iron) or turn pro. If you are a left-handed golfer it serves you right to be in Houston in June.

I would much rather be in Luling, Texas, on the twenty-sixth day of June when they hold their annual Watermelon-Thumpin' and Seed-Spittin' Contest. I am not as good at seed-spittin' as I once was, but as my golden years approached I developed into a gifted watermelon thumper. I've tuned my ear. With a slight, unobtrusive flick of an index finger (either one) I can gauge the degree of ripeness, sugar and moisture content of any watermelon.

By all means don't forget to observe June 25. On that fatal day, 111 years ago, Gen. George Armstrong Custer closed his colorful career in a blaze of glory. The legend says that before he rode into the valley of the Little Bighorn, he stopped by the Bureau of Indian Affairs Office and told them: "Don't do anything until I get back."

They haven't.

Dillon, Montana sits on the side of the Beaverhead River in the southwest corner of that magnificent state. At an elevation of 5,406 feet, it is a picture-book town of 5,000 souls with an economy rooted in stock raising, tourism, and Western Montana College.

Here, on a green grass and blue spruce campus, the central building of the college, Main Hall, rises from a native stone foundation, its stately red brick walls crowned with an octagonal tower. Since 1897, this tent-like structure has served as a symbol of learning.

But Dillon has other cultural resources and among them is the Eagle Bar.

My intellectual curiosity took me to this ancient tavern in downtown Dillon on a bright Montana morning. My first impression as I entered the grotto was how thoughtful either the architect or the bartender had been when he designed the floor plan. The well-worn hardwood bar extended to the front wall of the building so that a critical case of dehydration need not use his last ounce of body moisture before demanding replenishment.

The expert planning also provided a door at the far end of the bar to allow those who might encounter social pressures a rapid escape. The interior was scarcely illuminated by antique lights so as to camouflage the facial imperfections of the clientele. The decor was eclectic, running the gamut from beer clock ad modern to stuffed animal renaissance, delightfully diluted with auto parts calendars and a poster proclaiming the forthcoming Rotary Club fishing derby.

The staff, though efficient, was kept to a minimum, indicating the intent of the management to make a profit and not fritter away the cash flow on payroll and withholding taxes.

Indeed, the management and the staff may have been one and the same. She was a somewhat buxom lady with several gold teeth and a friendly face which invited fellowship, while at the same time demanded a degree of decorum. Two diamond rings on her left hand indicated she had at some time made the mistake of matrimony.

Her backbar was well supplied with regional ambrosia, her cooler case filled with the top ten beers of the backhoe crowd. Her expression mirrored many Montana winters and numerous confrontations with exuberant customers.

On the left side of the bar's entry way was a bulletin board containing several printed notices of community interest. I read them all carefully to inform myself on the character of the town. The Knights of Columbus were having a picnic on Labor Day; a county fair and rodeo were also on the calendar; a 4-H calf and sheep sale was scheduled; and a potluck dinner was billed at the American Legion Hall.

Then, one notice in hand-printed broad black letters caught my eye. Its message was so personal in nature I was surprised to see it posted in such a public place. I asked the bartender about it and she explained.

There had been a rather festive gathering a few evenings before and one of her regular customers had gotten a bit out of hand. This had created a domestic problem and the customer's wife and the management had resolved it by compromise. The mutual agreement was printed on plain, white paper and was there for all to observe. It reinforced my faith in humankind's ability to solve any problem; a blend of kindness, cooperation and compassion.

"No more drinks for Red Snodgrass after seven p.m."

There are those cynics who are convinced that our system of criminal justice has gone to the dogs. When I visited New Mexico two years ago, the direct benefit of that approach to the administration of justice was clearly demonstrated. I have many personal friends who are judges, so I don't wish to offend them. However, the New Mexico incident proved beyond a reasonable doubt that a well-bred German shepherd with sound teeth, should receive serious consideration when the government makes the next appointment to the bench.

When the City of Albuquerque abandoned a pueblo-type fire station on Central Avenue, it was purchased by a young man who converted it into an art gallery. A discerning man with both taste and substance, he filled it with fine Spanish Colonial furniture and stocked it with the works of well-known artists.

The location and reputation of the gallery attracted the carriage trade. However, these same attributes came to the attention of the criminal element of the city. The young man's gallery business did well, but he suffered a number of burglaries.

The police, lacking both prevention and detection ability as well as artistic appreciation, were totally ineffective. Electronic security systems were installed but were easily bypassed by experienced thieves. The break-ins continued. A friend suggested a guard dog.

He was beautiful: a well-trained beast with sharp white teeth, basic black coat, silver-tipped tail, broad chest and alert ears. One could detect a deep sense of duty in his demeanor. He roamed the property during the day, free and friendly, wagging his tail in the finest tradition of a solicitous salesman. At night he was left alone with only a bowl of water and responsibility. They named him Guggenheim.

Nothing untoward happened for several weeks. Each morning Guggenheim met his master with demonstrated delight. He was then given a modest breakfast and put in the yard for a run before resuming his daytime duties.

It was winter time when Guggenheim made his mark in life. The owner was met at the door by an excited Guggenheim. The gallery owner surveyed the scene. Not one bronze or oil was missing, but several pieces of furniture were tipped over and blood was everywhere.

Guggenheim was overjoyed and led his master to the second floor. More blood and many threads of what must have been a wool sweater were scattered about. On the third floor, still more blood and what appeared to be denim. The police theorized the thief had tried desperately to avoid the jaws of the German shepherd: then, in a last dash for life, dived through a second story window. After the police expressed sincere professional admiration for the skills displayed by Guggenheim, they checked local hospitals, but no dog-bite victim had appeared for treatment in their emergency rooms.

The police work was kept to a minimum. No trial burdened the county budget, or required the judge to cancel his plans to attend his class reunion. The legal atrocities of plea bargains and sequential appeals never were considered.

Now, Governor, give this some thought.

A few days ago I was engrossed in a novel, whose story line was set in a small town in the 1920s and early 30s. It was different from the usual ten-day productions that flood the market. The book contained a serious character study, nary a murder, no recreational sex... just enough to assure the family continuity. The bombshell in the story as far as I was concerned was the almost casual mention of a human fly. That really started my memory rolling.

What few human flies there are around the country today are big time. They no longer come to the small towns where there are no buildings more than three stories high. The only ones I have heard of recently have been a couple who climbed the World Trade Center in New York, but they used mountain-climbing equipment. The old-time human fly just walked up to a building with his feet in tennis shoes and his hands bare and started to climb right up the face of the structure until he got to the roof.

If the Downtown Prescott Association wants to attract a good crowd, bring back the human fly. When I was a boy the Prescott merchants used to hire a human fly every once in a while. Human flies traveled around the country like flagpole painters do. When one came to town, Black's Fish Market, Scholey's Pool Hall, Tilton's Music Store and the Green Lantern would be among those who would chip in to pay the fly.

I remember seeing the human fly climb the Head Hotel and the Tilton Building. I think I had the chicken pox when they climbed the St. Michael Hotel.

The merchants were pretty cagey. They never hired a human fly to climb a building on a Saturday because there would be plenty of shoppers downtown anyway. The fly was hired to perform on a weekday, usually about one or two o'clock in the afternoon. This made it mandatory for every kid in town to get food poisoning, pneumonia, or a ruptured appendix during the noon hour, so he or she could sneak downtown to see the human fly climb up the front of the building.

We would have great debates as to how the human fly managed to stick to the vertical surface. Some of the more shallow thinkers suggested he used suction cups or glue, but those of us who were more scientifically advanced were convinced the fly could cancel gravity.

No self-respecting fly would use a net. The daring and danger of the event was what brought the crowd out. They would not come downtown just to see a man fall into a net, but the possibility that you might be an eyewitness to a man splashing on the sidewalk, had a strong appeal.

I have no idea what caused the demise of the human fly. I consider it a great cultural loss. I have tried bird watching, But neither Blue Jays nor Tanagers have the color of a human fly.

Ruff Spots of Society

Well, the one-worlders are at it again. Such suspect organizations as the United Nations, Tri-Lateral Commission and Home Owners Coordinating Committee (HOCC) keep trying to erase borders to destroy national identity and make all people of the world into a single egalitarian society.

They have made considerable headway in the areas of dress, music and language. Anywhere in the world today it is the same. Everybody wears blue jeans and one-size-fits-all caps, plays hard rock and limits conversations to "have a nice day" and "you know."

Now this subversive movement is focused on cuisine to bring universal equality to the dinner table. I suspect the conspiracy will fail, for food loyalty is one facet of national heritage that cannot be obliterated. Social anthropologists tell us that the dietary barrier is the hardest one to break.

We willingly learn someone else's language, appreciate their music and adapt to living in their type of housing, but eat their food? No way. Farmer John would take a Chapter Eleven in Jerusalem, and bagels were never much in demand in Baghdad.

Much of North America was settled by the French, great lovers as well as great chefs. Yet French cuisine was never popular in this country until after World War II when it became chic. Even today, it won't play in Peoria.

Food has even become a political issue. In the 1840 presidential campaign, William Henry Harrison ran against Martin Van Buren. Harrison proudly proclaimed that he ate good, wholesome beef while his opponent Van Buren consumed such frail foods as cauliflower, celery and strawberries.

No one would vote for an eater of cauliflower, and rightly so. Harrison won. Unfortunately, he died one month after he took office.

President Bush used history to gain popularity, describing broccoli as about as appetizing as cod liver oil.

A few years ago, a Los Angeles firm, Lawry's Food, announced the opening of a taco factory in Ireland. If this succeeds, it is only a question of time before you see Guinness in Guadalajara. It is a plot to destroy nationalism.

I will never order escargots again. I did once and there was a snail in it. People are finicky about food. The first time an Irish tongue touches a pot of val verde chile, it will make Easter week in Belfast look like a Bolshoi presentation of *Swan Lake.* The Irish are a volatile, hot-tempered people but they will not eat anything spicier than a boiled potato. Irresponsible market invasion could create a world-wide food fight.

Of all the peoples of the world, the Spanish have been the most successful in establishing diet patterns on foreign soil. They introduced the production of citrus and wine to the California Indians. Those native Californians didn't cotton much to the orange juice but they sure lapped up the vino.

Although the Spanish have brought to our shores such gastronomical delights as roast piglet and paella, they must also take the responsibility for the environmental disaster of outdoor cooking. They brought the **barbacoa** to this then unsullied land. We know it today as the barbecue.

The food meddlers had better remember what the missionaries forgot. Food is like religion. Eat and believe anything you like but don't shove it down my throat.

The argument appears with the same alarming regularity as your power bill. The ill-informed always try to add sinew to their theory by the meaningless statement: "I know for a fact." In truth there is no fact. All we have are theories. "Gringo" is a common word in the Southwest. Once considered demeaning, it has evolved into nothing more than a benign ethnic term, no better nor worse than "Yankee." I heard a Nicaraguan spokesman use the expression on national television. I found it accurate rather than offensive.

I had a college roommate named Pancho Fernando Fontevilla. He was from Mazatlan, Mexico. His father was mayor of that city at the time and had considerable commercial interest. Pancho had attended prep school in the United States and spoke Spanish, French and English. He was well-mannered, kindly, a gentleman to the marrow of his bones. The first time we had an argument (a difference of opinion about a radio program) he called me a gringo. Having been called worse things than that, I took no offense but Pancho later apologized. Then we got into an argument about the source of the term.

Pancho insisted the term was first used at the time of the Mexican War. He claimed the American troops invading Mexico always sang the song written by the Scottish poet, Robert Burns, *"Green Grow the Rushes,"* hence the word Gringo.

The only poet I was familiar with at the time was cowboy Gail Gardner. But I "knew for fact" that Pancho was only half right. The Yankees in Mexico sang the song, popular at the time, *Green Grow the Lilacs* and it was from that the Mexicans coined the word gringo. Years later the musical *Green Grow the Lilacs* played on Broadway and the late Tex Ritter made his theatrical debut in that production.

When Pancho pressed me for more detail, I admitted I had no idea who had written it but certainly no poet from Scotland; it may damn well have been Gail Gardner. Pancho and I remained friends but my faith in his judgment was destroyed when he returned to his native Mexico and obtained the national franchise for Nash Automobiles.

Not that it is going to shake the academic world, but since that first international debate between Pancho and me, the real scholars have shed more light on the source of the word gringo. The best and the brightest claim it is a corruption of *griego* which means Greek. They point to the old Spanish expression, *Hablar en griego,* "to speak in Greek." The English equivalent is,"It's all Greek to me." This means, of course, it is foreign to our ears. The novelist Willa Cather mentioned in her classic, *Death Comes for the Archbishop* that "any European except a Spaniard was regarded as a gringo."

I never forgot the term. Years later, when I got a CB radio, I selected a call name, my handle, Gringo. By now Pancho would approve.

Headlines seldom declare the major changes in our lives. Frequently, the obscure wire feature foretells the trendy, the mutation in values, the next adaptation to contemporary life forced upon us.

Such a syndicated feature appeared the other day. Many of the major truck stops located on the interstates are selling a new product, a cologne for truck drivers. So far, two name brands have appeared on the market. Longhaul and Eighteen Wheels. I suppose the formula is secret, but a safe bet is that the base is a mixture of over-brewed coffee, NoDoz and diesel fuel. Maybe a little carbon monoxide.

Almost everybody wants to smell good but a team of British scientists have isolated a chemical substance from the sweat of human males that is so attractive to women it may be compounded into a new men's cologne or aftershave lotion.

Many of my generation not only shave daily but in our lifetimes have spent thousands of dollars on Caswell Massey, 4711, Bay Rum, English Leather and several brands of foot powder. Now the British scientists tell us this is all a waste. A woman prefers the perfume of male perspiration. This may explain the failures of my youth. Now, in my Sun City years, this message, like the message to García, arrives too late.

I intend to monitor a few truck stops and find out if the truck drivers have enjoyed an accelerated social life. The British announcement regarding the appealing qualities of male sweat may be a plot to reduce the American birth rate to zero. They are still a bit miffed about the outcome of the American Revolution. On the other hand, the sale and distribution of Longhaul and Eighteen Wheels bears close watching. If the truck stop waitresses start jumping over the counter when a road-weary, but scented, truck driver walks in, the English have lost again.

I can't believe that the British are right. Certainly, the average American woman is not turned on by a poorly ventilated locker room. If there was any truth in what the British say, Procter & Gamble long ago would have marketed gamy aftershave lotion and the Mennen Company would have had a perspiration cologne.

True, there are always exceptions. The misfits, maladjusted, the emotionally unstable. In my youth I knew two such cases. One was a young lady from Eloy. She seemed to get excited when she smelled a stagnant swamp cooler. The other was a graduate of the University of Arizona, born and raised on a cattle ranch near Fort Huachuca. Wet saddle blankets made her alarmingly aggressive. The truck drivers or the British, only time will tell who is on the right track.

Anywhere you go in the world today you will meet Americans. They are not the globe trotters the Japanese are, but they do move around a bit.

One of my daughters traveled all over Europe a few years ago and came home telling of meeting friends and friends of friends in tiny villages along the Adriatic Sea from Slovenia to Albania.

Today she still journeys frequently to cities in the United States and often runs into an Arizonan, Prescottonian or even a Chino Valleyan. Now she believes there are only sixty-seven people in the world.

Until recently, I was inclined to reject her thesis, but a visit to Maui convinced me she is right. I stayed on the west coast of the Hawaiian island, about twelve miles north of Lahaina, once a whaling village. Today, a museum is the only residue of this once-lucrative industry. Lahaina has abandoned harpooning humpbacks to zero in on visitors' Visa cards.

On Sunday morning I drove into town to attend

Mass. After receiving directions in three different dialects and five different routes, I finally found the parking lot. Across the street was the church, tall, graceful, colonial white.

Bingo is not permitted in Hawaii, but I noticed two nuns on the front lawn selling cookbooks, sea shell rosaries, stationery and votive candles, so I concluded this wasn't a Mormon church. It is the Maria Lenakila Church. The Franciscan priest led the procession to the altar wearing traditional vestments and a huge orchid lei.

His altar attendants wore either muumuus or Hawaiian shirts. The choir included native males and females, children, and those who were children decades ago. They sang in their native tongue and rhythm, accompanied by ukeleles and tambourines.

There were about 200 people attending the Mass, and in that Maui is a tourist Mecca, they were from all over the world.

The priest asked that everyone greet each other and tell where they were from. The young man sitting in front of me was from Globe, Arizona. After that coincidence was discussed (he knew a college friend of mine), I turned to the couple behind me. They were from Payson, Arizona. He was employed by Eddie Basha, knew my friends Don Dedera and Marguerite Noble. It was old home week.

Across the aisle was an attractive well-dressed woman. I thought perhaps, Tucson? Flagstaff? I asked.

Someplace in Southern France, she said.

I don't know anyone there.

I suppose when the daily subject matter you deal with is at least eight or ten centuries old, it removes you from or creates an indifference to contemporary life and any tool not made of bone, stone or rawhide.

My friend, a distinguished Southwestern archeologist, is a nearly normal individual considering he will trust nothing that can't be carbon-dated at 1,000 years old plus or minus 100 years. He purchased his field khakis when he was in graduate school from a war surplus outlet. He got a new car recently, but only because the transmission fell out of his Hudson Hornet right in front of Lou Grubb's Ford agency. He claims his old Underwood is dependable and continues to function every time the Palo Verde power station shuts down for a month or two. He does have a telephone (dial, not push-button). He converted his kitchen stove from wood to gas last winter. He thinks VCR is an epidemic disease.

Though he is well within the borders of Social Security, he is still much in demand for archeological clearances for land parcels. He writes, publishes and serves as a tribal consultant employed by several Indian nations and the law firms that represent them.

He was working recently on one of the most isolated Indian reservations in the Southwest, and after several days in the field had returned to his home study to write his reports. A perfectionist, he felt the need for more maps and documents. He knew the material was stored in a cardboard box in some jerry-built shelter deep within a remote canyon.

The time constraints worried him. He was familiar with the packhorse mail service in and out of the reservation, so he quickly wrote a note asking that the material be sent as soon as possible by the fastest type of carrier available. He knew what this would be—an ancient tribal pony lumbering up the ill-defined trail, an indifferent driver of a long-neglected pickup truck, and finally, a U.S. Postal Service as laid back and casual as the driver of the pickup.

Within twenty-four hours of mailing the letter to the tribal headquarters, my friend's phone rang. It was Mickey, the friendly Indian the archeologist had been working with. Mickey was direct and brief:

"Hey, Doc, we got what you want. What's your fax number?"

Suspicious of any three-letter word ending in x, the doctor asked, "My what?"

"Your fax number. We will fax the material to you right now."

"I don't have a fax."

Silence... then the archeologist heard Mickey whisper to the other members of the tribal council, "He ain't got no fax."

"No fax?"

"No fax!"

The tools of the tribe have at last surpassed those of the scientist. Now he's been thinking about getting a fax. And perhaps a microwave oven and maybe a cellular phone to put in his new Ford Explorer.

Bill Ahrendt
1980
©

CHAPTER

Ruff & Tumble of Politics

A friend of mine who runs a few head of cattle down near Aguila is in real trouble. The family ranch is a corporation. He is president, his wife, Hattie, is vice president and they have a son named Tweeker who isn't too smart so they made him secretary-treasurer. If they have a good year, plenty of rain, a good calf crop and three cows killed by the train, they go to Sea World in San Diego for a week. If it's a dry year and the train doesn't hit any of their cows, a long weekend in Nogales has to do.

My friend, Ingersol, opened his mail the other day as he does faithfully every month or so. Besides the hearing aid ads, an L.L. Bean catalog, an appeal from AARBC (Arizona Association for Retroactive Birth Control) and a nasty letter from American Express, there was a form to fill out and send in to The Help Keep Bob Stump in Congress Committee. Ingersol is what you call a conservative. He is opposed to a King holiday, the ERA, the *Washington Post* and hot tubs. Knowing that Bob Stump is a good ol' boy, he wrote out a check for $10 and was about to seal the envelope when he saw a notice on the back about election laws. It consisted of three simple sentences:

1. "The maximum amount you can contribute is $1,000 for the primary and another $1,000 for the general.

Your spouse can make a similar contribution."

This one didn't bother Ingersol. Ten bucks was all he was going to send but he resented the statement about having a spouse, as he has been true to his wife since two weeks before their wedding day.

2. "Only personal checks may be accepted. Corporate contributions are prohibited by law."

Ingersol figured that was no problem. He tore up the check which was printed: Calico Cattle Company, Inc. and was going to drive down and get a Circle K money order when he read line three.

3. "If you are a federal employee or if you have any matter pending before a federal regulatory commission or agency, please disregard this appeal."

This made Ingersol mad, so he wrote out another ranch check for $10 and sent it to Bob Stump to keep him in Congress. A few days ago when he went down to Phoenix he loked up his lawyer.

"You mean you sent Representative Stump a ranch check for his campaign?" inquired the counselor.

"Sure," said Ingersol.

"Do you still lease that land from the Bureau of Land Management?"

"Yep."

"Did you ever get that matter settled with the IRS about your 1988 taxes?"

"Not yet. We're still arguin' about it."

"Are you still trying to get a tombstone from the Veterans Administration for the Jim Gimbel grave at the ranch?"

"Well, I'm still tryin'. They sent me one, but they spelled his name wrong."

"Gimbel?"

"No. Jim."

"Do you still have the manure contract with the

EPA to supplement their hydroponic gardens at Morristown?"

"You bet I do. I deliver them a pickup load every other Monday."

"You, my friend, are in violation of the federal election laws," said the attorney. "Did your wife send a check too?"

"No. She's a political atheist. She wouldn't give a dollar to Billy Graham if he was runnin' for Mayor of Gisela."

"She's a wise woman," said the attorney.

A friend of mine, beloved for his instability and suspect because of his disaffection with the status quo, made an interesting observation the other day. Our court calendars are crammed with cases not worthy of the dignity and procedure of such a revered institution. These, of course, rob precious time better devoted to major issues.

He suggested some serious thought be given to bringing back the fine old American tradition of the duel. This would clear the court calendars, control population and be much more satisfying than a costly negotiated compromise which placates neither party and results in no permanent solution.

His case seems sound.

The method has an established historical precedent. Several of our presidents employed the duel to solve their differences. The result was sometimes conclusive, not to mention cheaper, quicker, and seldom appealed. True, the process does bypass the lawyers but that flaw of unemployment, he suggests, could be avoided by attorneys being available to serve as hired duelists representing individuals unschooled in firearms and unskilled in marksmanship. A modest fee would be paid for such representation.

The peripheral benefits are obvious. Anyone lacking reasonable ability in marksmanship and unable to afford a lawyer to duel on his behalf, could ask the court to appoint a skilled duelist who has passed the State Bar to represent him at county expense. The duel could be witnessed by an *amicus curiae* and the result entered into the court record. Such a system would serve society well.

Let me illustrate.

Two neighbors quarrel because one has a dog that barks all night. No need to hire a graduate harasser to write letters and threaten legal action suggesting a prolonged period of oral and written quibbling—which does nothing but generate ill feelings and burdensome expense. Simply schedule a duel at the appropriate time and place. All well-established homes would have an elegant burled walnut box containing a pair of dueling pistols. This weapon is much classier than an AK-47 and if mass produced could add considerably to our gross national product. If the dog owner wins the duel, this in effect would exonerate the dog and discourage the complaining neighbor in the future. If the complaining neighbor should win the duel, the dog would suffer the same fate as his master—a neighborhood twice blessed.

Crimes against society could be handled a bit differently. Such anti-social behavior as failure to signal, littering, joining the Sam Donaldson fan club, opening a subdivision and axe murder could result in the offender dueling with a court-appointed sharpshooter. This event could be self-supporting by advanced ticket sales.

The return of the dueling system is just around the

corner. Only one possible problem exists. Crimes which fail to generate public outrage such as selling real estate, cheating at golf, being a member of Congress and voting Republican...might go unchallenged and unpunished. No system is perfect.

Among the great losses we have suffered in recent years in the one-on-one quick retorts between political speakers and individual members of a hostile audience.

Unsympathetic audiences today are programmed to interrupt speakers they do not admire by chanting and stomping feet or mass booing rather than the individual barb. The ability of the speaker or his detractor to prevail has all but become a lost art.

The last such classic I can recall was during the 1960s when the late cartoonist Al Capp was paid well to face a campus gathering and tell the members of the radical left things they did not want to hear. At one such campus speech Mr. Capp made a statement one husky male member of the audience disagreed with, so he stood up and shouted "Bull——."

Capp never lost his stage presence. He looked at the detractor and replied, "Now that we have your name, what's your question?"

When Al Smith was a candidate for the office of President of the United States he was to give a speech to a rather unruly group. When he was introduced a member of the audience stood up and hollered: "Go ahead Al, tell them all you know. It won't take long." Smith smiled, looked at the man and replied. "If I tell them all we both

RANGERS
Bill Ahrendt

know, it won't take any longer." From that point on, Al Smith had the attention and support of the audience.

Not all speakers prevail in such verbal battles. Theodore Roosevelt, the twenty-sixth president of the United States, was a caustic and courageous public speaker. Following his graduation from Harvard in 1880 he studied law and served as a member of the New York Legislature. He was a writer, outdoorsman, police commissioner, soldier, assistant secretary of the Navy and finally President.

Roosevelt was a polished speaker with a nimble mind, but he became the victim of a rural wit when he was campaigning for governor in Upstate New York.

About half-way through his speech, building up to a stunning political crescendo, he was interrupted from the audience by a local celebrant who would periodically shout: "I'm a Democrat! I'm a Democrat!"

After about the third such exclamation Roosevelt spoke directly to the heckler and began to set the trap for his drunken adversary.

"May I ask the gentleman why he is a Democrat?" said Roosevelt. The heckler replied, "My grandfather was a Democrat; my father was a Democrat; so I'm a Democrat."

Then Roosevelt opened the jaws of his trap.

"My friend, suppose your grandfather had been a jackass and your father had been a jackass, then, what would you be?"

Instantly the drunk replied, "A Republican!"

It was a lesson Roosevelt never forgot.

The winter of 1903-04 had been a record one in isolated mining camp of Crown King, some 6,000 feet above sea level in the fabled Bradshaw Mountains. Waves of gray clouds skimmed the tree tops and snow fell on snow. Day after day the temperature never much rose above freezing.

The Crown Kingers stood close to their stoves until at last, it was April. Some shaded ice remained, but signs of spring and a warming sun cheered the camp.

It must have been that first hint of spring that caused the local justice of the peace to pet and embrace the female companion of Andres Bustamante in the camp's saloon that spring evening.

Judge G.A. Reynolds, not known for his sound judgment and great timing, showered his affection and biological intentions upon Bustamante's companion with total abandon. The result was predictable. Bustamante drew his pistol and placed a bullet completely through the thoriac cavity of Judge Reynolds.

Among his other deficiencies, the judge lacked youth. By the time he hit the board floor, he was dead. In a lot less time than it takes these days, Andres Bustamante was sitting in a stone cell at the Territorial Prison in Yuma.

There had been no plea bargain. Now with a busy summer coming on, Crown King was without a coroner or justice of the peace. The Yavapai County Board of Supervisors was willing to appoint somebody to the office, but no one in the mining community was willing to take the job.

By the time the November election was at hand, not a soul in the camp had declared his candidacy for the office. Then a camp character named "Bone Head" Hull filed the proper papers and was placed on the ballot.

The possibility of "Bone Head" presiding at the highest court in the Bradshaws, alarmed the locals. All

agreed that something had to be done to prevent this judicial disaster.

A day or two before the election, four hard rock miners were sitting around a table at Chung's restaurant drinking beer while waiting for the T-bone steaks that Chung was cooking on the iron surface of his wood stove. With beery voices they agreed that it was a crying shame that within hours, "Bone Head" Hull would be the law west of Bumble Bee.

In time, enough beer was consumed to make a sterling legal opinion possible. One of the hard rocks pointed at the others with the stem of his Peterson pipe and declared: "The law says that any office can be filled by a write-in candidate providing he gets the majority of the votes for the office in question."

The statement stood on the table like a Venus nugget while the possibilities were being silently sorted out. Just then, Chung came to the table with a tray of beef, cottage fried potatoes and sliced tomatoes covered with olive oil and vinegar. It was an omen.

As the steaks were placed on the table, one old miner said what all of them were thinking. "Chung, how would you like to be elected as justice of peace and coroner in these here parts?"

"What's matta, you have too much drink before you eat? You eat steak and potatoes!"

Then the cry. "Chung for justice of the peace! We can prove to the world that Crown King demands the best. We elect a man of intelligence, one with the wisdom of all the Orient, a direct descendant of Confucius. Chung for judge!"

The write-in campaign was a huge success. Sixty-three votes were cast. Chung got sixty-one, "Bone Head" Hull, two. When the results were final the citizens persuaded Indian Ed to open his saloon so a victory party for Judge Chung could be held. Both government and racial integration had come to Crown King.

The first six governors of the Territory of Arizona were Republican. Grover Cleveland broke the pattern when he was elected President in 1885. Cleveland appointed a Democrat, Conrad Meyer Zulick, who did not prove the greatest party asset since Thomas Jefferson. If President Cleveland had even glanced at Zulick's resume, he would have seen the signs of disaster. Zulick had a great background to prepare him for bank robbing and stagecoach holdups, but at the time, a politician was expected to possess other talents.

To begin with, Zulick had been a colonel in the Union Army in the War Between the States. He had also been a collector for Internal Revenue in Essex County, New Jersey, and had practiced law in Trenton.

Zulick had resided in Arizona only a year before his

appointment as governor of the territory. And when Democrats sought to congratulate him, Zulick was not to be found. After an extensive search he turned up in Sonora jailed for failing to meet the payroll of his Mexican mining ventures.

The Democrats made a decision. To wade through Mexican legalities, they determined, would be time-consuming, costly and embarrassing. They found their answer in an aging, but still effective, Army scout and undercover man, Doc Donovan. Donovan was hired. With a team and wagon, he crossed the border in the dark of night. Here history disagrees. Some insist Doc slipped by the jail guards, and others are convinced *mordida* (bribery) was the weapon a politician would normally turn to. In any event, Donovan put Zulick in the bed of his wagon, covered him with a canvas tarp and headed north. Only after he was in Arizona was Conrad Meyer Zulick informed that he was the first Democratic governor of Arizona.

What is Governor Zulick remembered for? Consider events of his administration. The rich Vulture Mine was sold shortly after Zulick took office. He owned no part of it, but received $20,000 from the proceeds of the sale. As governor, he placed four mounted tax collectors on the Arizona-Mexican border, to extract tribute on Mexican liquor, tobacco, horses, cattle, merchandise and more. No accounting of these collections was ever rendered. A year after Zulick was in office, all hostile Indians were pacified. Zulick took credit and insisted hostiles and friendlies alike be removed from their traditional homeland.

"I will not permit Arizona to become a breeding ground for assassins." he said.

Zulick's major atrocity is seared into the soul of the people of Prescott. He, more than any single individual, was responsible for moving the capital of Arizona from Prescott to Phoenix in 1889. That sacrilege has made it difficult for any gubernatorial Democrat candidate to carry Yavapai County since. The single exception was Bruce Babbitt, who promised he would bring the capital back.

My daughter called me the other day. She's the one who always refers to me as a Renaissance Redneck. In the past I have tried to call her on several occasions but an automatic answering device has made it impossible to communicate.

We haven't had a real daughter-father conversation since she was first runner-up for Rodeo Queen. I have given a lot of thought to buying one of those answering machines myself, but I am spending so much on birdseed it is out of the question. Since my cat suffered the loss of his ninth and final life, the birds are eating me out of house and hovel.

I never realized how just one aggressive cat could keep the bird population in check. The flip side of this sliver of the ecosystem is that I now buy about 400 pounds of birdseed a year. I have one sparrow here that must weigh eight and a half pounds. I don't need a watchdog. There is a blue jay around my place that makes Rambo look like a ballerina.

In the course of this benchmark conversation, my daughter wanted to know how old the State of Arizona was. It is so nice to give my children information after years of criticism of my grammar, spelling, and pronunciation.

The young lady seemed spellbound as I told her right off the top of my head that Arizona would celebrate a birthday on February 14. She questioned my answer, saying perhaps I had confused it with Valentine's Day. I assured her they were one and the same.

I further mentioned, in rather explicit terms, that in Arizona we celebrate the birth of our state, not an overly romantic holiday devoted to Cupid.

Arizona is a state, a system of law and government. Love, as any reasonable individual knows, is an emotional state of mind. Some unknown philosopher once observed, "Like the measles, love is most dangerous when it comes late in life."

As a native of this great state and proudly so, in spite of a couple of governors we have had, I plan to have *huevos rancheros* for breakfast, get my skin cancer touched up and wear my bola tie with the scorpion covered with clear plastic.

Remember, friends, we will all gather at noon, Wednesday at Governor George W.P. Hunt's tomb. Bring a six pack of A-1 Beer and wear your one-size-fits-all cap with the state flag patched on. The committee is going to furnish the tamales.

No red hearts now, or one of those cupids with a bow and arrow. Remember what Zsa Zsa Gabor said: "A man in love is incomplete until he is married. Then he is finished."

Emotion, manipulation, influence and fraud sometimes play a part in the democratic process of election. Crude and artless efforts such as vote-buying or ballot-box stuffing did exist in pre-computer days and many a good ol' boy went to Congress when the electorate had designated another destination.

While outright fraud cannot be condoned, the ability of a skilled manipulator, using the tools of quick wit and velvet deceit, stirs an admiration difficult to contain. One of these talented types lived in Prescott years ago, and his finest hour came in the election of November 3, 1896.

I have no idea what his legal name was. Everyone in Yavapai County knew him as Sandy Huntington. He was said to be a member of the well-respected California Huntington family presided over by Collis P. Huntington, one-time Sacramento merchant. Huntington, along with Leland Stanford, Charles Crocker and Mark Hopkins, became wealthy in railroading. Left as his memorial is the Huntington Library in San Marino, California.

Sandy was sent to Arizona by his family because of a severe drinking problem which had on more than one occasion been an embarrassment to his family. The Yavapai County sheriff gave Sandy a room in the livery stable and kept him busy with various odd jobs. Sandy had an above-average education for the times, and as a result, he often served on election boards and, as the law provided, as an aide for illiterate voters.

Because the sheriff served as a sort of patron saint for Sandy, their relationship was warm and friendly. The sheriff himself had some of the same character flaws as Sandy. His most recent term of office was sullied by several incidents of questionable behavior involving excesses readily encouraged by the various facilities of a frontier town.

Sandy, among others, considered the sheriff's reelection very doubtful. His opponent was well-known and respected and appeared to be free of transgressions the public attributed to the incumbent sheriff.

When Sandy reported to the polls early on election

morning, he was a worried man. He did, however, have the responsibility of acting as a voter's aid for the illiterates. None appeared until shortly after lunch. Sandy ushered the unschooled voter into the booth, drew the curtain and began to read aloud the ballot and to place an X when the illiterate indicated his preference.

The 1896 ballot had four parties represented: Republican, Democrat, People's Party (on which "Buckey" William O. O'Neill was running for territorial delegate to Congress), and the National Silver Party.

Five offices were voted before the team got halfway down the ballot and came to the office of sheriff. Sandy read it slowly and clearly. The People's Party and the National Silver Party had no candidates for sheriff, only the Republicans and the Democrats. He read:

"For sheriff of Yavapai County John S. Ross, Republican, George C. Ruffner, Democrat."

The illiterate, having heard the gossip about the sheriff, cried, "Ruffner? I don't want to vote for that S.O.B.!"

Sandy responded, "All right! We'll X that bastard out!"

The sheriff was reelected.

CHAPTER

Yarns with the Ruff Side Out

The word legend is frequently misused, but in the case of George McJunkin as he came to be known, it is both accurate and appropriate. George was born a slave on an East Texas plantation about 1856. The Civil War did little to disturb his status. He remained on the plantation where the owner, Jack McJunkin, took an interest in him.

McJunkin taught the lad to read and lent him books. George devoured them in his hunger to learn about the world around him. Then as a young man, he drifted west, honed in body and mind.

George took a job on a ranch near Midland, Texas, giving the name George McJunkin. His family name, if any, remained back on the East Texas plantation. In 1876, George McJunkin moved to Union County, New Mexico.

He was now a capable cowboy, an amateur geologist and the proud owner of a fine violin for which he had spent a year's wages. He became an accomplished fiddler and often entertained his companions with evening concerts.

In his saddlebags he always carried a small canteen, a bit of food and a couple of books. In a homemade saddle boot he toted a large telescope, never a gun. A gun, he reasoned, might be a source of trouble; a telescope might be a means of avoiding it.

George soon became the foreman of the Crowfoot Cattle Company. The owner was quick to see the character of George, rather than his color. The Crowfoot employed some twenty cowboys and covered a sprawling wilderness.

George McJunkin ran the spread with calm efficiency and assured self confidence. His dignity was never damaged, his orders never questioned. His decisions were arrived at by logic born of wisdom. He became a trusted confidant of the entire ranch family and made many critical decisions on their behalf. What few hours he rationed for his own interests, he spent with his books and violin.

On August 27, 1908, a record thunderstorm hit the Crowfoot. Thirteen inches of rain washed across the country. A tide of raging water roared down Cimarron Wash and destroyed most of the village of Folsom, causing several deaths.

A few days after the storm, George and one of his cowboys were inspecting the damage near Dead Horse Arroyo when they noticed large, white skeletal remains, fourteen feet below what had once been the top of the bank. Bleached bones are common in cattle country but George's knowledge and interest in antiquity stimulated his curiosity.

It must have taken millenia, he reasoned, for this much soil to cover what once was the surface of the earth. The bones were much larger than others George had examined; they must be ancient, he reasoned. Also found in the same stratum of soil were delicately crafted stone points, some imbedded in the bones of the animals.

The design of projectiles was much finer and the workmanship far better than those numerous arrow points which almost daily were picked up on the surface by the ranch hands. McJunkin's self-acquired knowledge of archaeology told him that this was a significant site. Science should be notified. It was generally believed at the time that North America had no early human occupation. The Folsom site, discovered by a self-educated, black cowboy was to prove otherwise.

George McJunkin kept several of the Folsom bones and points on the mantel of his fireplace until the day he died. When he closed his eyes for the last time, he was buried in the deep sand below the spring grass of the Crowfoot.

In time, science concurred with his thesis. The points were made by human hands. The bones of slain animals were at least ten centuries old.

A black man, plantation poor and born into slavery, made a significant scientific contribution, for he had learned to read, observe and reason.

© 1994 Bill Ahrendt

It was one of those unstructured relationships that have become part of today's society. Unencumbered by clergy, ceremony or clerk of the court, they shared bed and board agreeing to omit the vow 'til death do us part. It was his apartment and she became part of it.

He was a young attorney in Anchorage, Alaska, with a rapidly growing practice. She had her own career which permitted her the privilege of arranging fresh flowers for the dining room table on occasion, or sometimes, on Sunday mornings, surprising him with eggs benedict or other fine foods.

It was a comfortable life with all the joys of new matrimony, yet without the terrifying thoughts of ultimate alimony, child support payments and the terminal duet of spoon-counting and custody of the coffee pot. In time passion became dispassion, then personal habits and minuscule faults poisoned paradise.

When the young attorney had to travel to the Lower Forty-eight States on a business trip, he elected to take a straightforward, honest approach. He told his girl friend that the time had come for them to go their separate ways.

He was firm but reasonable. He told the young lady he would be gone for several days. She could take her time to pack and get out of the apartment.

He did insist, however that she leave the quarters clean and orderly. This, he suggested, was little enough to ask. She acknowledged the request with nothing but a nod. When he returned to the Anchorage apartment after several days, he was delighted to see that it was spotless.

The water bed was made up with clean linen, a favorite book had been placed on the nightstand and a chocolate caramel decorated the pillow. The mail had been placed on the hall table. There was not a spot of dust on any surface. The dishwasher was empty, the furniture dusted, every dish and table setting in its proper place.

A note on the refrigerator informed him that a prepared dinner awaited microwave heating. A single place setting was on the dining room table. The bathroom was immaculate. He had never seen the apartment so spic & span.

Then he sensed something wrong. A strange noise barely audible, came faintly to his ears. He checked the thermostat, windows, television, the appliances. Ah! There it was, the telephone was off the cradle. He picked it up and put it to his ear.

He heard a strange sound—a continuously replayed tape of a Japanese weather forecast emanating from Tokyo.

The attorney had no idea what the phone bill was going to total.

But he realized separations are seldom inexpensive.

Since that dreadful day, more than a century of sagas about little Charlie McComas have been printed. It is a sliver of Southwestern history, a touching story which has blurred vision with tears and fanned fires of hatred.

The final fate of Charlie McComas is still debated.

Charlie was the only child of Judge and Mrs. Thomas W. McComas of Silver City, New Mexico. Judge McComas was an attorney in private practice and he also served as chairman of the Grant County Commission. The judge had an extensive practice and numerous real estate and mining properties. At age fifty-seven, he looked forward to retirement to his well-stocked ranch at the headwaters of the Gila.

Juniatta McComas, twenty years younger than her husband, was a local beauty and prime mover for the social and cultural betterment of Silver City.

On the afternoon of March 28, 1883, Judge McComas hitched two fine horses to a new buckboard, and with Charlie and his mother and a picnic dinner, headed southwest toward the Burro Mountains to inspect a mining property and enjoy a family outing. Weeks before, Chato, a renegade Apache and terrorist of the time, had left his camp in Mexico to raid American camps in the north, and to replenish his camp larder which was depleted by war and winter.

Chato's raids had gained him little. Four Mexican woodchoppers were slaughtered in the Huachuca Mountains, but there was little loot. A few days later, Chato and his band killed two miners in the Winchester Mountains northwest of Wilcox. That camp, too, provided few spoils.

When Judge McComas and his family did not return home by Tuesday evening, a search was begun. After several days the scene of their last supper was found. A rider came upon a bloody tablecloth and discarded picnic basket. The Judge's body had been shredded by several shotgun blasts, then beaten to a pulp with boulders. Juniatta McComas' frail skull was crushed. The horses and little Charlie were not to be found.

An extensive police and military search for Charlie proved fruitless. Rumors about six-year-old Charlie sprouted like alfileria on a damp desert: he had been sold into slavery in Mexico; adopted by an Apache family; he lived in the Sierra Madres in Mexico; or he had been murdered with his mother and father, his body hidden by boulders; he had escaped from Chato but died of thirst and exposure. Citizens of Silver city collected $1,000, went to Mexico and offered a ransom. Nothing.

As late as 1920, the Mexican Army reported that a bearded Anglo was the leader of a band of Apaches and Yaquis who raided a mining camp a few miles south of the Arizona border.

Charlie McComas?

In 1936, when Charlie McComas would have been nearly sixty years old, an archaeological expedition from the University of Illinois went into the Sierra Madre Mountains of Mexico. They found an isolated camp of Apaches living in primitive conditions. In this group of Indians, living as they did, was an old white man with a long, reddish beard.

Charlie?

Certainly, by now the bones of Charlie McComas are buried or burned. He sleeps under the same blanket of earth where his mother and father found peace.

He was one of those happy, outgoing, but mentally slow individuals who lived in the blurred world of fantasy. Very few people in Globe, Arizona knew his full name. He appeared in town about 1920. Within weeks, he knew everyone in the town and all his new friends called him Scissor Bill. Not one of the better intellects in Gila County, nevertheless he was a high-profile member of the community and beloved by all. Scissor bill displayed a number of commendable character traits. He lived modestly, and was never known to drink, smoke, cuss, or express a desire to attend law school.

Forty-some-odd miles northwest of Globe, construction began on Roosevelt Dam in 1905. Six years later, it was dedicated. To take advantage of the dam's recreational lake, Gila County built a road from Globe, through the Webster Mountains.

Friends often took Scissor Bill along when they went to Roosevelt Lake for the day, but he never waded in the water or wet a line, preferring to entertain his hosts by telling tall tales about the wild west. That was bill's fantasy world.

One summer morning in 1923, Harley Snover was grading the country road about halfway between Globe and the dam. Harley had the grader's blade lowered and was creeping along the road, trying to smooth out the bumps. As he approached a gentle curve a strange figure appeared from behind a high boulder. Harley, a native of Globe, had no difficulty recognizing Scissor Bill. Bill held a six shooter in each hand; a red bandanna covered his lower face. His huge black Stetson was pulled down on his head to eye level. His pants were tucked into the legs of his black cowboy boots. Pointing both pistols at the grader operator, Scissor Bill blared the message through his bandanna:

"All right mister! Throw down the strongbox!"

"The what?"

"Now don't try nothin' funny," said Bill, "throw down that strongbox there by your foot."

"Hell, Bill, that ain't no strongbox, that's just my lunch bucket!"

"Don't try and fool me, fellow, give me the strongbox!"

The driver stopped the grader and stepped down on the road, lunch pail in hand.

"Here, see for yourself, Bill," he said, as he handed the bandit the open lunch bucket.

Scissor Bill looked, grinned, pulled his bandanna down around his neck and holstered the two pistols. The two men talked, exchanged a little Globe gossip, then sat down together beneath a single shade tree and devoured Harley's lunch.

Allowing three or four weeks to pass in order to separate crime from punishment, the county grader operator reported the incident to his superiors. They, in turn, well aware that Scissor Bill was two flakes short of a full bale, declined to press charges.

Those of us who are irrevocable romantics like to think of the incident as the last stagecoach robbery recorded in the annals of Arizona history.

We owe Scissor Bill that much.

The big white snowflakes fell silently, steadily, hushing the sounds of the little town of Prescott. Inside the warm wood structure of Cob-Web Hall, a game was in progress. As was his custom, a quiet new citizen sat without expression in a comfortable captain's chair. With agate-like eyes he gazed at the green felt table top, never betraying the quality of his cards.

He had appeared in town only a few weeks before and soon became a habitue of the town's finest saloon. People wispered about his past. The rumor was that he had killed a man in a tent saloon at a railroad construction site, but frontier ethics discouraged inquiry. He was obviously a gentleman, soft-spoken, well mannered and impressive in appearance. Always tastefully dressed, here on Block 13, which later would be called Whiskey Row, he had found a home.

So intense was the game no one but the bartender noticed the entry of a stern-faced, sixtyish man into the saloon. He walked unhurriedly, directly to the card table and with a liquid motion drew his revolver and shot the patrician gambler twice. With the same regal walk he left the saloon, mounted his well-bred horse and galloped south on Montezuma Street. At the edge of town he crossed Granite Creek and disappeared into a second growth of timber. Soon events would suggest a theory: a father avenging a wronged daughter.

No one claimed the body of the gambler. His few new friends had no idea where he had been living. He had come to Cob-Web Hall every day as a gentleman enjoying his private club. But beyond his talents at the table, little was known.

A few weeks later, Captain Fisher was preparing to close his Cob-Web Hall for the night when he noticed a strange package at the end of the bar near the door. Folding back the clean linen he discovered a beautiful brown-eyed baby girl and a still-warm nursing bottle. The timing was poor. The saloon was about to be closed and here was an infant to care for.

Captain Fisher, true to his trade, had an answer. Everyone would ante $10 for a roll of high dice, the winner would become a temporary father with funds to care for the child until something could be done.

The first few rolls were unimpressive. Finally, Bob Groom, the surveyor of the townsite, rolled four fives. A cheer went up and premature congratulations were offered the engineer-bachelor. But Judge Charles Hall, a cultured man devoted equally to his childless wife, William Shakespeare, and the gaming tables, protested that he had not yet rolled the dice. He was granted a turn. And from the Judge's well-manicured hand four sixes fell on the green felt table.

Cheers again and congratulations, toasts of French champagne. Bob Groom suggested that as runner-up, he should be given the privilege of giving the girl a name.

The men nodded. He raised his crystal glass and announced—Chance Cob-Web, and of course, the family name, Hall.

Judge and Mrs. Hall adopted the waif, raised her and gave her a fine education, following a fruitless, exhaustive search to locate her mother. Prescott families lost track of the young lady after she went away to school and the Halls died.

Some twenty years later, a prominent, elderly Prescott attorney met a charming young couple at a San Francisco dinner party. When the young matron learned the attorney was from Arizona she remarked that she had been born in Prescott and asked him if he knew the town. Indeed he did.

"Did you know my father, Judge Hall?" she inquired.

"Yes, very well. He was held in high esteem in Prescott."

"What, my dear, is your name?" the attorney asked.

"It's an odd one," the young lady replied. "When I was in school, everyone called me C.C. It really is Chance Cob-Web. My father was fascinated with the West and I suspect it comes from some fantasy of frontier life, for he was quite a student of the subject."

The old man's jaw muscles tightened and his eyes glistened bright and moist, but he held his tears.

"Yes, I suppose," he said, "it must have been something like that."

Sekaquaptewa is a name which does not roll easily from even the most agile Anglo tongue. Hopi indian from the heart out, it is an honored name that has been identified with agriculture, publishing, tribal government, law and academia.

The various members of this distinguished family are catholic in their interests and all have made significant contributions to their tribe, state and country.

When the Korean War erupted , Emory Sekaquaptewa was a student at the University of Arizona studying anthropology. He was active in the ROTC program. So it followed that he was commissioned as a lieutenant in the U.S. Air Force and went on active duty. He served as a line officer and in administration. One of the bases he was assigned to was at Greenville, Mississippi, north of Vicksburg, on the Mississippi River near the Arkansas border.

It goes without saying that the slow, syrupy southern tongue had some difficulty with his name. Between Greenville, Mississippi and the pueblo village of Hoteville, Arizona, there exists a substantial cultural gap.

In his own squadron, however, the more conscientious personnel were first attracted by this exotic name, then went to work to learn to pronounce it properly. One major in Emory's squadron, when he first encountered the name Sekaquaptewa on the roster, expressed some desire to retire from the military; but being a determined soul, he set about to conquer, and ended up fluent in Hopi, at least in that one word.

The major learned to pronounce the name flawlessly and was very proud of his accomplishment. And well he might be; I have known many Air Force majors who never achieved such an advanced skill in their entire careers. The major did have a degree of frustration, however, for in Greenville his ability went unnoticed, Sekaquaptewa having become a name almost as familiar as Yancy.

A weekend training flight soon offered the major an opportunity to flaunt his talent. The flight to Jacksonville, Florida was uneventful and as soon as the flight plan had been closed, the crew went downtown to take in the sights. An elegant bar and dining room in a posh hotel appealed to the five officers. Dressed in their best, the men entered the facility and were shown to a table.

After a long wait, which seems mandatory in such places, an indifferent but efficient waiter approached their table. The background music was soft and tasteful and the waiter seemed to move to the table as if waltzing to a well-rendered Strauss composition. A crisp, white linen towel was draped over his left forearm.

After greeting the group with a cheerful, "Good evening, gentlemen," he inquired if they might want something to drink. The major, being the ranking officer, replied, determined to stump this perfectionist.

"Yes, please," he said, "we would like five Sekaquaptewas."

The waiter replied, "Certainly."

Within minutes, five tall, chilled glasses festooned

with lemon and cherries were delivered to the table on a silver tray.

On those all-too-rare, but delightful times when I see my friend, Emory Sekaquaptewa, distinguished professor and jurist, I have often asked him what kind of drink it was. Emory answers honestly.

"I don't know. I think it may have been vodka and something like Seven Up, maybe rum, I don't know."

If I ever get to Jacksonville I'm going to order a Sekaquaptewa.

With my luck, I'll get my face slapped.

The founder and first editor of *The Miner,* predecessor to today's Prescott daily journal, was the always vocal and often volatile John H. Marion. Marion abhorred political expediency and typographical error, both of which outlived him.

Marion was a community leader, and when the new commanding general of the Military Department of Arizona arrived at Fort Whipple, Prescott, Arizona Territory, in July, 1870, it was the colorful John H. Marion who met him, interviewed him and advised him on how he should discharge the duties of his new command.

Gen. George Stoneman, always the gentleman, a courteous audience, heard Marion urge total genocide of the American Indian. Stoneman thanked Marion for his observations, expressed a desire for an enduring friendship and politely ignored his advice.

Stoneman was born in Busti, New York in 1822 and graduated in 1846 from West Point. He served on the western frontier prior to the Civil War as a junior officer.

During that time he became an accomplished cavalryman, led numerous raids, and fought gallantly at Fredericksburg. Captured near Clinton, Georgia in August, 1864, he was exchanged to withdraw from additional field duty.

To nurture the friendship between press and miliary, Stoneman invited Marion on an extensive inspection trip of the Military District of Arizona. Marion, more at home in a captain's chair than a soldier's saddle, courageously accepted the general's invitation.

The detail departed Whipple August 29, 1870. Marion was the single civilian among twenty-five enlisted men and officers. They went to Camp Verde, skirted the San Francisco Peaks, visited Camp Goodwin and Camp Bowie, went west to Tucson, stopped at Florence and Fort McDowell, marched northwest via Castle Hot Springs to Date Creek, then returned home to Fort Whipple.

General Stoneman's report to the War Department called for closing seven installations including Fort Whipple. He also recommended that Camp Date Creek become a major garrison. What had been a strong cable of friendship between Stoneman and Marion now turned to twine. Marion, outraged, wrote an extensive and caustic article in *The Miner* disagreeing with the Stoneman report and casting some doubt of the acuity of the military mind.

Within the year, political pressure and the scandal of the Camp Grant Massacre of Indian women and children brought about General Stoneman's retirement. He retreated to his ranch in the San Gabriel Valley of California. He soon became railroad commissioner of California, and a decade later was elected governor to serve a four-year term.

Sixty days in an Army saddle did little to dull the pen of John H. Marion. When he published his diatribe in his newspaper, he ran 700 extras and sold them out at fifty cents a copy, a price unheard of at the time.

Today there are three known copies of the issue existing in archives. They are found in the Sterling Library, Yale University Library, New Haven, Connecticut, the Denver Public Library, and the Huntington Library, San Marino, California.

Although virtually unknown among newspaper editors, John H. Marion must have mellowed a bit before he went to that great newsroom in the sky.

He crusaded by editorial and other strong measures to name the only natural lake in the territory in honor of the general. This small body of water, formed eons ago as a volcano, had been known as Chavez Lake.

Today, Stoneman Lake it is. The general and the editor had reached a point of accord.

One August day, 1880, on the dirt streets of Prescott, Arizona Territory, Albert, the six-year-old son of local merchant Louis Wollenberg, was run over by a freight wagon and killed.

The family, of Jewish faith, had come to Prescott from California, the father in 1874, Mrs. Wollenberg and the children, two years later.

At the time of Albert's death there was no synagogue in Arizona, so Michael Goldwater, uncle of Senator Barry Goldwater, delivered the funeral address in Yiddish. Every Prescott business, including the saloons, closed for the sad event as little Albert was buried in the Masonic Cemetery.

An account of the Wollenberg family and their life in Prescott a century ago was published in the October,

1982 edition of the *Western States Jewish Historical Quarterly*. The quarterly, produced under the auspices of the Southern California Jewish Historical Society, drew upon a memoir of Charles M. Wollenberg. Charles was three years old when he accompanied his mother to Prescott.

Mr. Wollenberg's story of his childhood desert journey and his life in Prescott is a classic. One portion of his tale, dealing with the honesty of a child and the imposition of values, I found both humorous and poignant. He tells of attending a Methodist Sunday School in Prescott when he was eight years old.

One Sunday morning, a visiting minister spoke to the class about the evils of alcohol. The minister placed pictures on the wall of the room. One image showed a human liver in healthy condition, because, the minister said, it had never been poisoned by intoxicating liquor. Beside this was a picture of a liver in deplorable condition, due, the minister said, to the drinking of alcohol.

The traveling clergyman then emptied a box of attractive badges onto the table and asked the children to pledge they would never let liquor touch their lips. As each child vowed, the cleric would give an award.

Little Charles Wollenberg paused, then, remembering something about his family and the past, he began to cry. The Sunday School teacher tried to comfort him. What was the problem? Charles asked if port wine was intoxicating, if it contained alcohol. When he was answered affirmatively, he told his story.

When he was three years old and crossed the desert with his mother, brothers and sisters from the Colorado River to Prescott, a water barrel on the wagon fractured and lost its contents. On the third day out the children began to suffer from thirst.

Mrs. Wollenberg remembered she had a basket of port wine for her husband. She opened it and soaked her handkerchief in the wine to let the children suck the moisture-laden linen. That port wine and his mother had saved his life. Now with tears streaming down his cheeks, he declined to take the pledge.

Charles M. Wollenberg was born March 13, 1873, in Castroville, California. He graduated from Prescott High School and attended the University of California at Berkeley, where he obtained a degree in pharmacology. After a long career as a druggist and civic servant in the San Francisco area, he died in 1949 at age of seventy-six.

When he wrote his article for the Jewish journal he said, "I didn't take the pledge that day in Sunday School. I still haven't."

His home is in upscale Paradise Valley, but he doesn't dress the part. He is seldom seen in a blue blazer and button-down shirt, prefers pickups to Porsches, and would rather be riding a horse on his ranch.

William Howard O'Brien is a graduate of the University of Arizona; he is a farmer, cattleman, horseman, businessman. A lifetime outdoors together with an Irish ancestry have given him a macrame face not unlike that of Ronald Reagan.

His eyes have weathered well. They sparkle and reveal intelligence and humor, a combination required to survive in today's world.

Cattle, crops and the crap game we call business keep Bill O'Brien busy. Yet he still finds time for his talented tomfoolery. He is the most creative practical joker in Arizona. O'Brien's bag of tricks never demean or hurt the victim, but they have been known to confuse, excite and create fantasies ending in gross, hilarious reality.

One dark, stormy night Bill's wife was out of town so he set aside an evening to entertain a few friends, all men. About twenty good ol' boys gathered at Bill's home.

It was to be a simple get-together, a few drinks, a steak dinner and some windies told by the local Lotharios. Right after the second drink, the doorbell rang. Bill rushed to the door.

There, somewhat damp but beautifully dressed, was a stunningly gorgeous woman on the verge of tears. In a most cultured voice, she apologized for the intrusion and explained that her car had broken down. She wished to call a tow truck.

O'Brien, the solicitous, said he would retire to the kitchen and place the required call. In the meantime, would the lady like a drink to ward off the chill?

"Yes, please, a brandy."

After serving the lady, Bill retired to the kitchen, supposedly to telephone. What he did was seat himself at a vantage spot to watch the action.

The lady drank her brandy, and removed her hat and coat. One of Bill's guests, now well-removed from reality, poured her another. Then she coquettishly kicked off her high heals. Most of the ol' boys shifted in their seats and stole side glances at each other.

A few froze, appearing to be made of marble. She smiled, suggested the brandy warmed her too well, then removed her suit coat and blouse. O'Brien's joy was unrestrained as he watched his caper from the kitchen.

A bit more brandy and off came her skirt and slip. Mass fantasy had now reached full gallop. Half of the guests were palsied and the others, overly optimistic.

As soon as her bra hit the floor, William Howard O'Brien came in from the kitchen and mercifully stopped the charade. He gathered the lady's clothing, escorted her to the dressing room and assured her the taxi was waiting for her as he had promised.

The evening's entertainment cost him several dollars. He figures the money was well spent, and that the friends forgave him when he finally got around to putting the steaks on the grill.

There are those who still speak of her in whispered tone. They lower their eyes to their gnarled hands and almost inaudibly surrender a coaxed comment regarding her power to heal.

Their mothers and fathers swore she was a brown-skinned saint with divine power to make well the sick and cause the blind to see again. In her native Mexico she was regarded as royalty in the Yaqui tribe before her people had been expelled from the country.

At the turn of the century she had come with her parents to the valley of the Upper Gila River and there she continued to minister to the Mexican families whose tortilla winners labored in the mines. They knew that if she would come to them their babies would not die and their aged would escape pain. She was only twenty-two when she came to Clifton, Arizona. She closed her warm brown eyes when she placed her strong hands on the heads of the afflicted and intoned her prayers.

She and her family lived in a remote area which afforded seclusion and the quiet required for meditation.

As the fame of "Saint Teresa" grew, more and more Mexican families sought her out and begged that she come to their homes to heal their ill. She always refused payment for her saintly service but her father frequently remained after she departed. Rumors flourished that he accepted a fortune in fees.

In the conduct of her calling, Maria Teresa met the handsome young José Rodríquez. The romance bloomed and soon a wedding date was set for late August. The thought of a saint entering matrimony was most distasteful to her followers. They offered prayers that such a sacrilege would never come to pass. On the wedding day a mob of the Mexican faithful gathered at the church in Clifton. When the ceremony was over the new bridegroom was arrested by the authorities on a charge of insanity. Escorted by her parents, Maria Teresa left at once for Los Angeles. Arizona's only "saint" never returned.

In the valley of the Upper Gila there are still a few very old ones who patiently wait for her. Even the warm sun no longer eases the pain in their bones and the light which comes to their eyes grows dimmer day by day.

Because of his excessive lifestyle and brutality in battle he is not remembered fondly in the American mind. He died at age eighty-one in Mexico City in 1876.

For the last two years of his life he lived in poverty and neglect. For a man who loved gaudy uniforms, abundant food and drink, intimate relationships and national adoration, it was a sad last chapter. Yet, when we scan the pages of history, few if any, individuals in a role of leadership have ever matched his colorful career.

António López de Santa Anna—a general, president and dictator—was born in Jalapa, Mexico. His family were people of modest means and scant ambition. Not António.

He was aware that a miliary career was the rapid route to social, political and economic standing.

At the age of twenty-seven, he led his first revolt against Emperor Iturbide in 1822. This was the first of three revolts led by Santa Anna. He became president of Mexico for the first of four times in 1833.

He is, of course, best known for his conquest of The Alamo in San Antonio, Texas, and his defeat and capture by Sam Houston a month later at San Jacinto. That military disaster and disgrace would have written the end to most careers, but not that of Santa Anna.

He was recalled from one of his three exiles in 1847 and made president and commander of the Mexican Army defending Mexico against invasion by the United States troops. He suffered defeats in three major battles and was driven from Mexico City by General Winfield Scott.

Again, Santa Anna was exiled, again recalled, once more made president and once more recalled in 1855. Between 1855 and his final return to his native land in 1874 two years before his death, Santa Anna had lived in Venezuela, Cuba, St. Thomas, Virgin Islands, and Staten Island, New York.

Why New York? As a business representative, the general brought a sample of chicle, the latex of the sapodilla tree, a native of southern Mexico and Central America. Natives there chewed the chicle. The old general wanted to develop a product market.

He found a customer, Thomas Adams, a New York grocer. The first marketed chewing gum was sold in unflavored balls. Sales were modest, for chewing without flavor or food value was considered foolish.

Not until 1880, four years after the general slipped into his final sleep, was chewing gum given a flavor... licorice. Adams Clove Gum and Dentyne followed.

General, president, dictator. António López de Santa

Anna is remembered as a man who captured The Alamo. He should also be remembered as the man who exported the joys of chewing gum to the world.

Santa Anna never became a Mexican Wrigley. He never owned an island in the Pacific, a baseball team or a winter mansion on a desert hill in Arizona. He died huddled in a dank Mexico City cellar.

His mother and father were rural school teachers when they first met. A few years after they married, Bob joined the faculty of the College of Agriculture at the University of Arizona.

They raised two sons. One attended law school and became a prominent Arizona attorney. The other, my friend, pursued a sort of quasi-profession closely related to the agricultural interests that were apparent in the family.

The two brothers are quite different. The older one, the lawyer, is handsome, trim and possessing of a quiet dignity. He has met with success in both his public and private life.

The other, my friend, is a big man, tall and wide, with a deep chest and an abdomen that is rapidly surpassing it. He speaks not softly, and in lieu of dignity, he displays a zest for life and people, with humor free of ostentation.

Living in a small town a few miles from the Mexican border, he is fluent in Spanish and profane in English. I see him infrequently, but that is not a disadvantage, for like aged bourbon, just a taste lasts a long time.

I don't really know how many times old Jim has

been married. I have met three of his wives and the one I met just recently might be number five. But let's hope for the best and say she is only *cuatro*.

Our recent visit was typical, unplanned, as guests at a friend's ranch. I heard him before I saw him. He was sitting beneath a shade tree with an attractive woman I had never seen before. He was near the foot traffic of the other guests as they moved about, giving him the opportunity to greet each one as if he were the host, running for office, or both.

Unable to delay any longer the joy of old Jim, I walked over to where he and his lady companion were enthroned. We men greeted each other as blood brothers. That ceremony concluded, I bowed, nodded, or knelt toward the woman seated next to him.

She was delighted to bask in his obvious, if somewhat regional, prominence. Finally, taking my cue, Jim spoke.

"Budge, I want you to meet my wife...Barbara Jean." This name I could not recall. I remembered Vicky, Carol and Margo. There may have been one or two others with whom I never crossed paths.

I acknowledged the introduction, saying only, "Happy to meet you."

Jim then mentioned they had recently been married and were adjusting to the new role after a strained period of getting to know each other. I didn't press for details.

"We got off to kind of a funny start," said Jim, "I thought *she* had money and she thought *I* had money. By the time we both found out, the damage had been done."

Forty miles northwest of Fort Apache, within the borders of the White Mountain Apache Reservation, is Cibecue. It was near this traditional encampment on August 30, 1881, that a happening transpired, tragic in itself and in its consequences.

The Apaches, then well contained, were mesmerized by Nokay Delklinne, A Coyotero medicine man conducting ghost dances. These ceremonials, he assured them, would result in the return of Diablo, the renowned Apache warchief. Diablo, the medicine man promised, would lead all Apaches to total victory over their enemy—the white man.

Col. Eugene Asa Carr road out of Fort Apache, Arizona with six officers, seventy-nine troopers and twenty-three Indian scouts to arrest Nokay Delklinne and prevent hostilities. Three hundred enraged Apaches shadowed the column. When Carr was bivouacked for the night, his own Indian scouts opened fire on his position.

Captain Hentig was the first casualty, but the troop gathered their forces a short distance downstream on Cibecue Creek and soon controlled the situation. Ten troopers had been killed and forty-seven Apaches taken prisoner.

For the next two months, sporadic warfare flared between the soldiers and the Indians. This resulted in the capture and court-martial of five Apache scouts who had mutinied at Cibecue. They went on trial at Fort Grant. Two privates, known only as Number Eleven and Number Fifteen, were dishonorably discharged and imprisoned at Alcatraz military prison in San Francisco Bay. Number Eleven got eight years and Number Fifteen, five. The remaining three, including Sergeant Dead Shot, were sentenced to be hanged. Throughout the territory, Indians decried the harshness of the sentence. The military was unmoved.

On March 3, 1882, the three Apache mutineers together dropped through the single gallows trap. That same day, the wife of Dead Shot hanged herself from a tree at San Carlos. The two small sons of Dead Shot and his wife were now orphans, ages eight and five. Confused and shocked, they knew not what to do.

The only real home they had ever known was the family camp at Fort Apache. It took the boys two weeks to walk from San Carlos to Fort Apache. When they arrived at the abandoned wickiup and the cold ashes of the family fire, they were naked and half-starved.

Unable to find food or blankets, the boys went to the telegraph office where the telegrapher, Will C. Barnes, who later won a Congressional Medal of Honor, was on duty. Barnes summoned Lt. Charles G. Gatewood, who four years later was to accept Geronimo's surrender at Skeleton Canyon. Lieutenant Gatewood ordered rations, blankets, clothing and shelter for the two boys. Dead Shot had scouted for Gatewood and was well regarded by the lieutenant.

Four months later, Gen. George Crook returned to Arizona arriving at Fort Apache, July 1882. Crook rode a large gray mule, and wore a yellow canvas coat and pith helmet. As was his custom, he was armed only with a double-barreled, sawed-off shot gun.

Greeted by the Apaches as "Shal-e-man" (friend), Crook was told about the two orphans camped at Fort Apache. The soldiers had named one of the boys Riley, but the younger one retained his Apache name, Na-Pas. Crook assigned quarters to the boys and had them tutored by the sutler's wife and various enlisted personnel. Both Riley and Na-Pas proved to be good students. They became fluent in English and proficient at mathematics and composition, all of which was to serve them well in the future.

When the two sons of Dead Shot entered manhood they were well prepared to serve their people. They saw a nonproductive reservation rich in grass, water and varied topography, ideal for beef production. Both brothers urged their tribal leaders to become involved in the cattle industry. After several false starts, a fine breeding herd was established. Today, the White Mountain Apache Herefords rank among the best.

Now the bones of Riley and Na-Pas rest in their native soil near Whiteriver. Men like Crook and Barnes are the genuine heroes of history. Not because they fought Indians, but because they saw in them the potential of peace and prosperity.

Ruffly Settling Up

The title page of this book states that I wrote it. That's not entirely accurate. It took more years than I want to admit, and about the same number of helpful personalities to pull this off. My support system is extensive and diverse, from cowboy and Indian to artist and archeologist. An oldtimer I knew some years ago was in the habit of visiting everyone he owed, to pay them personally in cash every spring and autumn after he had sold his cattle. He told them he wanted to "settle up."

So do I. I have no more valued friend and creditor than Don Dedera, my publisher. A mutual friend of ours, a man himself of many talents, is convinced that Don is a genius. While that may or may not be true, I can testify that Don is a fine and gifted human being. Don's pardner in the Prickly Pear Press is Designer Randy Irvine. Hell, Randy may be the genius in that outfit.

Jim Garner is the newspaper editor who first foisted me off on the public. I can't speak for the public, but I am grateful to Jim for the time and ink he has squandered on me. The words in this book are graced by the sketches of Bill Ahrendt. Bill may be the premier painter of the West working at the easel today. I am indebted for his images, which illuminate a text in ways a writer cannot.

Every life structure, however modest, requires a foundation. For many of us that foundation was a teacher. So it was with me. In my last two years of high school Lenore Childress, English teacher, introduced me to distinguished world literature. She also appreciated regional humor, and faulted me not when I attempted to compose some of it.

If I really were to settle up, I would have to thank profusely a hundred and a half good ol' boys and four splendid women. I don t even remember the name of the graybearded mountain cowhand I conversed with in Pie Town, New Mexico, but he has my gratitude for adding insights to my trip and words to my vocabulary. Many of my revered cronies have made their last ride away from the fire. Gail Gardner, cowboy poet, comes to mind. With him I roamed Arizona and the West in a Ford pickup. A graduate of Dartmouth, Gail flew Army biplanes in Texas during World War I, and he often boasted that no German aircraft got past El Paso. Nowadays I'm left with a kindred spirit, Dr. Robert C. Euler, to ride shotgun when I hit the trail.

The woman in my professional life is Jonne Markham. She has edited my copy for thirty years. It was impossible for her to fix all the split infinitives, dangling participles and misplaced prepositions, so numerous were they. But she tried. Gracias, Jonne, gracias.

Finally, I have known every one of the nineteen governors of the State of Arizona. For them, mil gracias! They were not always worthy of admiration, but ever rich in material.

Budge Ruffner
Alone in the Sierra Prietas
November, 1994

 THE INDEX: A RUFF TALLY 

RUFF DATA

Ruff Country text is set in 12-point Stone Serif,
with chapter heads and initial letters
set in Bodoni Poster, a typeface
ruffly as old as Gutenberg himself.

The paper is a seventy-pound Springhill,
ruffly what the publisher could afford.
There is nothing ruff about the printer,
Century Graphics, or the softcover bookbinder,
Central Bindery, both of Phoenix, Arizona.

Of the first edition, 110 copies
were reserved for a limited, numbered,
collector run bound in a ruff cloth
by Roswell Bookbinding of Phoenix,
and signed by the author.

For those who lost out
on the hardbound version,
well, life's ruff.